I0843328

# Tears of the Titans

Barry Robbins

# Dedication

To Pam, my caregiver extraordinaire, without whom this work would not have been possible. Words cannot express my gratitude.

For all sad words of tongue and pen, The saddest are these, 'It might have been'.

John Greenleaf Whittier

# Contents

# Prelude

Regret. It is a feeling that knows no bounds, a haunting specter that lingers in the hearts and minds of all who have dared to dream, to love, to strive for something greater than themselves. It is a universal human experience, one that transcends time and place, culture and circumstance.

In the pages that follow, we will embark on a journey into the very heart of regret, as seen through the eyes of some of history's most fascinating and influential figures. From the halls of power to the frontiers of discovery, from the battlefields of war to the stages of revolution, we will explore the profound and often painful moments that have shaped the lives and legacies of these remarkable individuals.

Through a series of intimate, first-person narratives, we will delve into the minds and souls of those who have grappled with the weight of their own choices and actions. We will hear their stories in their own words, feel the depth of their emotions, and come to understand the complex tapestry of factors that have led them to their greatest regrets.

But this is not merely a collection of historical curiosities or cautionary tales. Rather, it is an exploration of the very nature of the human condition, a testament to the power of our decisions and the indelible mark they leave upon our lives and the world around us.

By illuminating the regrets of these towering figures, we hope to shed light on the universal struggles and triumphs that unite us all. For in the end, it is not the achievements or accolades that define us, but the way we grapple with our own failings and learn from the mistakes of the past.

So let us embark on this journey together, and in doing so, perhaps find a new understanding of ourselves and the complex, beautiful, and ultimately human experience of regret.

# Chapter 1

# Galileo Galilei

# The Recantation of Truth

The quill trembles in my weathered hand as I dip it into the inkwell, the parchment before me a stark reminder of the choice I must make. I, Galileo Galilei, once a champion of truth and reason, now find myself at the mercy of the Holy Office, forced to choose between my convictions and my own survival.

As I sit in the dimly lit chamber, the weight of my years bearing down upon me, I cannot help but reflect on the path that led me to this moment. From my earliest days, I was consumed by a hunger for knowledge, a burning desire to unravel the secrets of the universe. Through countless hours of observation and experimentation, I sought to pierce the veil of ignorance and superstition, to shed light on the true nature of the cosmos.

And yet, as I stand on the precipice of my greatest triumph, I find myself haunted by the specter of my own demise. The Church, once a beacon of enlightenment and learning, has become a bastion of dogma and intolerance, deaf to the evidence of the senses and blind to the beauty of the natural world.

I think back to the moment of my greatest discovery, the realization that the Earth revolves around the sun, a truth that flew in the face of centuries of religious doctrine. With trembling hands, I penned my treatise, "Dialogue Concerning the Two Chief World Systems," a work that I believed would usher in a new era of scientific understanding and intellectual freedom.

But instead of accolades and acceptance, I was met with scorn and persecution. The Inquisition, that shadowy arm of the Church, descended upon me like a pack of ravenous wolves, determined to silence the voice of reason and preserve the status quo.

And now, as I face the ultimate test of my faith and my integrity, I am torn between two impossible choices. To recant my beliefs, to deny the evidence of my own eyes and the conclusions of my own mind, would be to betray everything I have ever stood for, to surrender my very soul to the forces of darkness.

But to stand firm, to cling to my convictions in the face of certain doom, would be to condemn myself to a fate worse than death. The rack, the stake, the slow agony of the dungeons—these are the tools of the Inquisition, the price of defiance in a world ruled by fear and superstition.

In the end, I know that I must choose survival, that I must bend to the will of my persecutors and recant the truth that burns within me. With a heavy heart, I put quill to parchment, my hand shaking as I scrawl the words that will haunt me for the rest of my days.

"I, Galileo Galilei, hereby abjure, curse, and detest the error and heresy of the motion of the earth..."

As the ink dries on the page, I feel a part of myself wither and die, the light of reason extinguished by the darkness of fear. I know that I will carry this shame, this regret, to my grave, a burden too heavy for any man to bear.

But even as I submit to the will of the Church, I cannot help but whisper the words that have become my mantra, my secret rebellion against the forces of ignorance and oppression.

*"Eppur si muove."*

"And yet, it moves."

For in the end, no matter how hard they try to suppress the truth, no matter how many voices they silence or minds they crush, the universe will continue to unfold according to its own immutable laws. And someday, perhaps long after I am gone, the light of reason will shine once more, and the sacrifices of those who fought for it will not have been in vain.

# Chapter 2

# Tomas de Torquemada

## The Grand Inquisitor's Confession

The flames crackle and roar, consuming the heretic's body. The smell of burning flesh mingles with the incense that fills the air, a sickeningly sweet aroma that clings to my robes like a curse. I watch the scene unfold, my face impassive, my heart hardened by years of relentless pursuit of purity.

Yet, in this moment of triumph, a flicker of doubt ignites within my soul. Is this truly the will of God? Are these flames a testament to my unwavering faith, or a grotesque spectacle of cruelty and fanaticism?

I have dedicated my life to rooting out heresy, to purging Spain of those who would defile the true faith. I have presided over countless trials, witnessed the agonies of the accused, and condemned many to a fiery death.

I have justified my actions in the name of God, convinced that I am fulfilling a divine mandate to protect the Church from the insidious influence of those who would undermine its authority. But as I gaze upon the burning pyre, a gnawing doubt begins to consume me.

Have I gone too far? Have I become the very thing I sought to destroy? A monster, a tyrant, a man consumed by the flames of his own righteousness?

The screams of the condemned echo in my ears, a haunting chorus of pain and despair. Their faces contorted in agony, their bodies writhing in the flames, a gruesome testament to the depths of human suffering.

I try to block out the images, to focus on the righteousness of my cause, but the doubt persists. It gnaws at my soul, a relentless reminder of the blood that stains my hands.

I remember the words of the Gospel: "Love your enemies, do good to those who hate you, bless those who curse you, pray for those who mistreat you." Yet, I have shown no love, no mercy, no compassion to those who have strayed from the path of righteousness.

I have become an instrument of fear, a symbol of oppression. My name is synonymous with cruelty, a chilling reminder of the dark side of faith.

As the flames die down, leaving only ashes and the lingering stench of burnt flesh, I am left with a profound sense of emptiness. The victory feels hollow, the righteousness tarnished.

In the depths of my soul, a flicker of regret ignites. Perhaps, in my zeal to protect the faith, I have lost sight of its true meaning. Perhaps, in my quest for purity, I have become corrupted by the very evil I sought to eradicate.

But the doubt is fleeting, quickly extinguished by the flames of fanaticism that still burn within me. I have gone too far to turn back now. I must continue my holy mission, even if it means sacrificing my own humanity in the process.

For in the end, I am convinced that my actions are justified, that the ends justify the means. The salvation of souls is at stake, and I will not rest until Spain is cleansed of the heretical taint that threatens to consume it.

# Chapter 3

# Marcus Junius Brutus

# The Bitter Fruit of Tyrannicide

In the flickering light of my tent, the ghosts of the Ides of March swirling around me like the ashes of a shattered dream, I, Marcus Junius Brutus, sit alone with my thoughts, haunted by the memory of the deed that has brought me to this bitter end.

The blood of Caesar, my friend, my mentor, my benefactor, still stains my hands, a crimson testament to the terrible price of my own misguided idealism. In my arrogance, my blind devotion to the ideals of the Republic, I convinced myself that his death was a necessary sacrifice, a noble act of liberation that would save Rome from the clutches of tyranny.

But now, as I sit here on the eve of my own destruction, the last remnants of my once-proud army scattered to the winds, I cannot escape the sickening realization that I have been a fool, a pawn in a game of power and ambition that I never truly understood.

I think back to that fateful day in the Senate, the cold steel of the dagger in my hand, the look of shock and betrayal in Caesar's eyes as I plunged the blade into his flesh. "Et tu, Brute?" he gasped, his final words a searing indictment of my own treachery, a reminder of the sacred bond of friendship and loyalty that I had so ruthlessly betrayed.

In that moment, I truly believed that I was acting as a true Roman, a defender of liberty and the rule of law. I had convinced myself that Caesar's growing power and popularity posed a mortal threat to the very foundations of the Republic, that his ambition would lead to the destruction of all that we held dear.

But even as I struck the fatal blow, I could feel the weight of doubt and uncertainty bearing down upon me, a gnawing sense that perhaps I had been too hasty, too easily swayed by the honeyed words of Cassius and the other conspirators.

For what kind of republic had we truly saved, if our actions had only plunged the city into chaos and civil war? What kind of liberty had we defended, if our noble cause had been so easily hijacked by the likes of Antony and Octavian, the very men who now sought to destroy us?

I think of the long months of struggle and sacrifice that followed, the bitter campaigns and bloody battles that have left me broken and defeated. I think of the friends and allies who have fallen by my side, the brave men who believed in our cause and paid the ultimate price for their loyalty.

And I cannot help but wonder if their deaths, and my own impending doom, are the just punishments for my own hubris and folly. For in my zeal to save the Republic, I fear that I may have only hastened its demise, that my actions have paved the way for an even greater tyranny to come.

The irony of it all is almost too much to bear. In trying to prevent the rise of a dictator, I may have only cleared the path for one far worse than Caesar ever could have been. In striking down a man I once called friend, I have lost everything that ever truly mattered to me—my honor, my integrity, my very sense of self.

And now, as the enemy closes in and the final reckoning approaches, I am left to ponder the bitter fruit of my own misguided actions. The ghost of Caesar haunts my every waking moment, a silent reproach for the betrayal and bloodshed that I have unleashed upon the world.

Perhaps, in the end, that is the true price of tyrannicide—the knowledge that in seeking to destroy a monster, we risk becoming monsters ourselves. That in our rush to defend the ideals of the Republic, we may only succeed in tearing it apart from within.

These are the heavy thoughts that weigh upon me as I prepare to meet my fate, the regrets that will follow me into the eternal darkness. But even in my despair, I cling to one last shred of hope—the hope that perhaps, in some small way, my own tragic tale may serve as a warning to those who come after, a reminder of the terrible consequences of unchecked ambition and the perils of political violence.

And so, as I take my final breath and the darkness closes in around me, I offer up a prayer for the future of Rome, for the preservation of the values and institutions that I once held so dear. May the gods have mercy on my soul, and may the Republic that I fought and died for endure long after my own name has faded into the mists of history.

# Chapter 4
# King Henry VIII
# The Hollow Crown

In the fading light of my royal chambers, I, Henry VIII, King of England, Lord of Ireland, and Supreme Head of the Church of England, find myself alone with the weight of a lifetime of choices bearing down upon my weary soul. The trappings of power that once brought me such joy and pride now feel like chains, the burdens of a king who has sacrificed much in the pursuit of his own desires and ambitions.

I think back to the early days of my reign, when the world seemed a vast and glittering prize, ripe for the taking. I was young and strong, a true Renaissance prince, skilled in the arts of war and diplomacy, the darling of the court and the people alike. I believed that I could bend the very fabric of history to my will, that I could shape the destiny of my kingdom with the force of my own indomitable spirit.

But now, as I feel the weight of years pressing down upon me and the shadow of mortality looming ever closer, I am forced to reckon with the consequences of my actions, the toll that my choices have taken on those around me and on the very soul of my nation. I think of the women who shared my bed and my throne, the wives who bore me children and the ones who felt the sharp edge of my wrath. Catherine, Anne, Jane, Anne, Catherine, Katherine: each of them a tale of love, loss, and betrayal, a testament to my own inconstancy and cruelty.

I thought I was doing God's work when I broke with Rome and established myself as the Supreme Head of the Church of England. I believed that I was freeing my people from the tyranny of a foreign power and the corruption of a decadent clergy. But now, as I survey the turmoil and unrest that my religious policies have unleashed, I cannot help but wonder if the price of my pride was too high. The monasteries dissolved, the treasures of the church seized, the blood of martyrs staining the streets—all for what? A legacy of division and strife that will plague my kingdom for generations to come?

And what of the men who served me, the advisors and confidants who helped me navigate the treacherous waters of statecraft? Thomas More, Thomas Cromwell, Thomas Wolsey—each of them a brilliant mind and a loyal servant, each of them brought low by my own capricious will. I thought I was ridding myself of those who would thwart my desires, but in truth, I was only isolating myself further, surrounding myself with flatterers and yes-men who would tell me what I wanted to hear, even as my kingdom crumbled around me.

But perhaps my greatest regret is the legacy that I leave for my children, the sons and daughters who will inherit the weight of my crown and the consequences of my actions. Edward, my long-awaited male heir, so young and frail, ill-prepared for the burdens of kingship. Mary, my daughter by Catherine of Aragon, her heart hardened by years of rejection and humiliation at my hands.

Elizabeth, my daughter by Anne Boleyn, a fierce and brilliant girl, but one who will have to fight for her very survival in a world that is hostile to women in power.

I wanted to be remembered as a great king, a ruler who brought glory and prosperity to his people. But now, as I face the end of my days, I fear that my legacy will be one of division and strife, of a kingdom torn apart by religious conflict and political upheaval. I have sown the seeds of my own destruction, and it is my children who will reap the bitter harvest.

But perhaps it is not too late for redemption, for a final act of wisdom and grace in a life too often marked by folly and cruelty. If I cannot undo the mistakes of my past, then let me at least strive to make amends in the time that remains to me. Let me seek to heal the wounds that I have inflicted on my people and my family, to build bridges where I have sown division, to plant the seeds of a better future, even if I will not live to see the fruit of my labors.

For in the end, the true measure of a king is not the wealth of his treasury nor the might of his armies, but the love and loyalty of his people, the strength and stability of the kingdom that he leaves behind. And though my own reign may be remembered as one of tumult and strife, let it also be said that in my final days, I sought to make things right, to leave a legacy of hope and healing for the generations to come.

# Chapter 5

# Wolfgang Amadeus Mozart

## Requiem for a Dream

In the echoing halls of eternity, where the celestial melodies of the ages play on in endless harmonies, I, Wolfgang Amadeus Mozart, find myself lost in a swirling tempest of regret and longing. The music that once flowed from my pen like water from a fountain now haunts me with its unfinished strains, the ghostly echoes of a life cut short by the cruel hand of fate.

I think back on my brief journey through the mortal realm, a flickering candle that burned too brightly, too quickly. From the moment I first drew breath, music was the very air I breathed, the language of my soul. The keyboard was my voice, the orchestra my canvas, and the world my stage. But even as I reveled in the accolades and the adoration of the court and the public, I could not escape the gnawing sense that time was slipping through my fingers like so many grains of sand.

The operas, the concertos, the symphonies—each one a jewel in the crown of my creation, a testament to the boundless riches of my imagination. But for every work that sprang fully formed from my mind, there were a dozen more that haunted my dreams, melodies that danced just beyond my grasp, tantalizingly out of reach.

I think of the Requiem, my final opus, the great unfinished masterpiece that was to be my ultimate legacy. Even as I lay on my deathbed, wracked with fever and delirium, I could hear the choirs of angels singing in my mind, the thunderous drumbeats of the Dies Irae, the plaintive strains of the Lacrimosa. But the cruel irony of my fate was that I would not live to see it completed, to hear my own voice joined with the celestial chorus in that ultimate symphony of the soul.

And then there were the earthly struggles, the petty rivalries and jealousies that dogged my every step. The court intrigues, the backstabbing and the betrayals, the constant scramble for patronage and prestige. How much of my precious time and energy did I waste on these trifling matters, these insignificant squabbles that seemed so important in the moment, but that now fade into nothingness in the face of eternity?

I think of my father, my dearest Leopold, the man who gave me life and music, but who also burdened me with his own dreams and expectations. The letters, the endless hectoring and criticism, the constant reminders of my duty and my destiny. I loved him with all my heart, but there were times when I felt suffocated by his presence, when I longed to break free and chart my own course, to be my own man and my own master.

And then there was Constanze, my beloved wife, my muse and my anchor in a turbulent world. How I regret the times I neglected her, the moments of tenderness and companionship that I sacrificed on the altar of my art. The children we lost, the tears we shed, the quiet desperation of a love stretched to the breaking point by the demands of genius and ambition.

But perhaps my greatest regret is the music that I will never write, the symphonies and operas and concertos that will forever remain locked in the vault of my imagination. The world will never know the full measure of my gift, the depths of my soul that I poured into every note and every phrase. And that, more than anything, is the true tragedy of my life, the unfinished symphony that will haunt me for all eternity.

And yet, even in the midst of my sorrow and my regret, I cannot help but feel a sense of gratitude and wonder at the sheer beauty of the music that I was privileged to bring into the world. The joy on the faces of the audiences, the tears in their eyes as they listened to my melodies, the way my music touched something deep and primal in the human soul—these are the memories that I will cherish forever, the moments of grace that made all the struggles and the sacrifices worthwhile.

And so, I will continue to compose, to pour out my heart and my soul in an endless symphony of regret and redemption. For in the end, that is all any artist can do—to give voice to the unspoken longings of the human spirit, to capture the fleeting beauty of the world in all its terror and its glory, and to leave behind a legacy that will echo through the ages, long after the last note has faded into silence.

This is my gift, my burden, and my eternal regret. But it is also my greatest joy and my deepest fulfillment. For in the music, I have found the meaning of my life, the purpose of my existence. And though the candle may have burned too quickly, though the symphony may remain unfinished, I know that the melody will play on forever, in the hearts and minds of all who have been touched by the magic of Wolfgang Amadeus Mozart.

# Chapter 6

# Antonio Salieri

# The Discord of a Life in the Shadows

In the fading twilight of my years, I, Antonio Salieri, once the most celebrated composer in all of Vienna, find myself haunted by the specter of a legacy forever eclipsed by the brilliance of another. The name that falls from every lip, the melody that echoes through every hall—Wolfgang Amadeus Mozart, the wunderkind, the divine prodigy, the one whose very existence has cast a pall over my own life's work.

I think back to those early days, when I first heard whispers of this young upstart from Salzburg, a mere child who could coax the most heavenly sounds from a keyboard with the ease of a master. I dismissed the rumors as idle chatter, the exaggerations of a fickle public always eager for the next sensation. But when I finally laid eyes on him, when I witnessed the effortless grace of his compositions and the adoration of the court, I felt a chill run through my very soul.

Here was a talent that surpassed my own in every way, a natural facility for music that I had spent a lifetime trying to cultivate through hard work and discipline. And yet, even as I marveled at his genius, I could not suppress the twinge of envy that gnawed at my heart, the bitter realization that I would forever be relegated to the role of a footnote in the annals of musical history.

I think of the countless hours I spent honing my craft, studying the great masters and striving to create works that would stand the test of time. The operas, the concertos, the sacred music—each one a testament to my own skill and dedication, an offering to the muses that I hoped would secure my place in the pantheon of the greats. But even as I basked in the applause of the audiences and the favor of the emperor, I could not shake the feeling that I was living on borrowed time, that my success was a fleeting illusion destined to crumble in the face of Mozart's ascendancy.

And so, I found myself locked in a desperate struggle to maintain my relevance, to prove to the world and to myself that I was more than just a competent craftsman, but a true artist worthy of the highest accolades. I poured my heart and soul into every composition, pushing myself to new heights of innovation and expression, even as the specter of Mozart's genius loomed ever larger on the horizon.

But for all my efforts, I could not escape the cruel reality of my own limitations. Where Mozart's music flowed like water from a spring, effortless and pure, mine was the product of endless toil and revision, a pale imitation of the divine spark that animated his every note. And as the years passed and his fame grew, I found myself increasingly consumed by a sense of bitterness and despair, a corrosive envy that ate away at my very soul.

I think of the whispers that began to circulate in the later years, the rumors that I had played some nefarious role in Mozart's untimely demise. The very idea was ludicrous, a vile slander born of ignorance and malice. But even as I protested my innocence, I could not help but feel a perverse sense of satisfaction at the thought that my name would forever be linked with his, even if only as a villain in the drama of his life.

And now, as I approach the end of my own journey, I find myself consumed by regret—not for any imagined crime or conspiracy, but for the way in which I allowed my own jealousy and insecurity to poison the well of my creativity. I think of the works I might have written, the collaborations I might have forged, the joy I might have found in the simple act of making music, had I not been so consumed by the need to prove myself in the face of an impossible standard.

But perhaps my greatest regret is the realization that, in the end, my rivalry with Mozart was a hollow one, a shadow play of my own making. For he was not my enemy, but my mirror, a reflection of the divine spark that animates all true artists, regardless of their fame or fortune. And in my blind envy and resentment, I failed to see the beauty and the truth that lay at the heart of his music, the universal language of the soul that transcends all earthly boundaries.

And so, I am left to ponder the bitter irony of my own legacy, the fact that I will forever be remembered not for my own achievements, but for my association with a man whose greatness I could never hope to match. But perhaps there is a strange sort of comfort in this, a recognition that even in the face of our own limitations and failures, we are all part of a larger tapestry, a grand symphony of the human experience that will endure long after our individual voices have faded into silence.

For in the end, what is any artist but a vessel for the divine, a humble servant of the muse that moves through us all? And if my own role in that great cosmic drama was to be the counterpoint to Mozart's melody, the shadow that threw his light into sharper relief, then perhaps that is a legacy worth embracing, a gift to the ages that I can offer with a full and grateful heart.

So let history judge me as it will, let the whispers and the rumors swirl around my name like leaves in the wind. For I know that in the grand scheme of things, my own petty jealousies and regrets are but a small and fleeting thing, a discordant note in the great symphony of life.

And though I may never know the peace and the joy that Mozart seemed to find so effortlessly, I can take solace in the knowledge that I, too, have played my part in the great drama of human creation, and that somewhere, in some far-off corner of the universe, my music will live on, a testament to the enduring power of the artist's spirit, and the eternal struggle to wrest meaning and beauty from the chaos of existence.

# Chapter 7

# James Madison

## The Perils of Compromise

As I look back upon the great work to which I devoted so much of my life, the Constitution that has guided our nation through more than two centuries of triumph and trial, I, James Madison, find myself burdened by a sense of unease, a realization that even the most noble of intentions can be tainted by the harsh realities of compromise and concession.

I think back to those sweltering summer days in Philadelphia, as the delegates to the Constitutional Convention debated and haggled, each fighting for the interests of their own states and factions. I remember the ideals that drove us, the lofty visions of a republic founded on the principles of liberty, equality, and justice. But I also remember the compromises we made, the deals we struck in the name of unity and expediency, and I cannot help but feel a twinge of regret.

The Three-Fifths Compromise. Even now, the words taste bitter on my tongue. I, who abhorred the institution of slavery, who saw it as a stain upon the soul of our nation, found myself complicit in its perpetuation. We counted each slave as three-fifths of a person, not to diminish their humanity, but to appease the Southern states, to bring them into the fold of our new Union. But in doing so, we enshrined the very evil we sought to eradicate, and we set the stage for a conflict that would tear our nation apart.

I think of the generations of African Americans who have suffered under the yoke of oppression, of the blood spilled in the Civil War, of the long and painful struggle for civil rights that continues to this day. And I cannot help but wonder if we could have done more, if we should have stood firm against the forces of injustice, even at the risk of our own dreams of unity.

But slavery was not the only compromise we made. I think of the ambiguities in our language, the phrases left open to interpretation and dispute. The right to bear arms, the powers reserved to the states—these were the products of careful negotiation, attempts to balance competing interests and ideologies. But in our desire for consensus, perhaps we sacrificed clarity, leaving future generations to grapple with the consequences of our equivocation.

I think of the debates that have raged throughout our history, the arguments over the scope of federal power, the boundaries of individual liberty. I think of the Supreme Court, tasked with interpreting the words we crafted, and I wonder if we placed too heavy a burden on their shoulders. Did we give them the tools they needed to navigate the changing tides of our society, or did we saddle them with a document that was, by its very nature, a product of its time?

And then there are the rights we left unprotected, the freedoms we assumed but did not explicitly enshrine. The right to privacy, the right to education—these are the values we hold dear, but they are not the ones we chose to codify. Perhaps we assumed too much, trusted too deeply in the wisdom of future generations to recognize the importance of these liberties. Or perhaps we simply lacked the foresight to anticipate the challenges our nation would face.

As I reflect on these shortcomings, these moments of compromise and concession, I cannot help but feel a sense of responsibility, a weight of regret that we did not do more to build a more perfect Union. But I also know that the Constitution we created was not meant to be a static document, a fixed and immutable set of laws. It was meant to be a living thing, a framework that could adapt and evolve with the needs of our society.

And so, even as I grapple with the consequences of our compromises, I find solace in the knowledge that the work of perfecting our Union is never truly finished. It is a task that falls to each generation, to build upon the foundation we laid and to strive always towards that more perfect ideal.

The genius of our Constitution lies in its capacity for change, its ability to bend and grow with the arc of history. And though we may have fallen short in our own time, though we may have made compromises that haunt us still, I have faith that the enduring principles we enshrined—of liberty, of justice, of the rule of law—will continue to light the way forward, guiding our nation ever closer to that shining city on a hill.

So let us learn from our mistakes, let us strive always to do better, to be better. But let us also take pride in what we accomplished, in the great experiment in self-governance that we set in motion. The Constitution we created is not just a set of rules and procedures—it is a testament to the enduring power of the human spirit, to our capacity for reason and compromise, for hope and progress.

And that, my friends, is a legacy worth cherishing, a foundation upon which to build a future brighter than any we could have imagined. The true brilliance of our system lies in its potential—the potential for growth, for change, for the constant pursuit of that more perfect Union.

# Chapter 8

# Thomas Jefferson

## The Anguish of a Conflicted Enlightenment Mind

In the flickering candlelight of my study at Monticello, amidst the books and papers that chronicle a life dedicated to the pursuit of liberty and justice, I, Thomas Jefferson, sit alone with my thoughts, tormented by the specter of the great contradiction that has haunted my every waking moment.

As the author of the Declaration of Independence, I enshrined the words "all men are created equal" as the very foundation of our new nation, a beacon of hope and freedom for all who yearned to break free from the shackles of tyranny. And yet, even as I wrote those words, I knew in my heart that I was living a lie, that the noble ideals I espoused were but a mockery of the reality that surrounded me.

For I, Thomas Jefferson, the champion of liberty, was also a slaveowner, a man who bought and sold human beings as if they were mere property, who forced them to toil in my fields and labor in my household, all the while denying them the very rights and freedoms that I claimed to hold so dear.

I think of the faces of those I have enslaved, the men and women and children who have suffered under the yoke of my hypocrisy. I see the pain in their eyes, the silent accusation that haunts my every waking moment, the knowledge that for all my high-minded rhetoric about freedom and equality, I have been complicit in the most terrible crime imaginable.

There was a time when I convinced myself that slavery was a necessary evil, that the economic prosperity of the South depended on the forced labor of the Negroes, that gradual emancipation was the only practical solution. But even as I clung to these feeble justifications, I knew in my heart that they were but a flimsy veil, a desperate attempt to reconcile the irreconcilable.

For how could I, a man of the Enlightenment, a believer in the fundamental dignity and worth of every human being, justify the ownership of my fellow man? How could I speak of liberty and justice, of the inalienable rights of life, liberty, and the pursuit of happiness, while denying those very rights to the people who toiled in my own fields and households?

I think of the missed opportunities, the chances I had to take a stand, to use my influence and my position to push for abolition, to set an example for others to follow. But time and time again, I fell short, allowing my own economic interests and political ambitions to trump the dictates of my conscience.

Even in my personal life, I failed to live up to the ideals I espoused. The relationship I had with Sally Hemings, the enslaved woman who bore several of my children—this was a betrayal not only of my principles but of the trust and dignity of the women I claimed to love.

As I reflect on the shame and the sorrow of my life as a slave-owner, I cannot help but feel a profound sense of regret and despair. For all my accomplishments and accolades, for all the stirring words I penned in defense of liberty and justice, I know that my legacy will forever be tainted by the blood and tears of those I held in bondage.

And yet, even in the depths of my anguish, I cling to a faint hope that perhaps, in some small way, my own struggles and contradictions may serve as a cautionary tale for future generations, a reminder of the terrible price we pay when we allow our ideals to be compromised by our own self-interest and weakness.

For if we are to build a true republic, a nation of laws and not of men, we must be willing to confront the hard truths of our own history, to acknowledge the sins of the past and work to build a more just and equitable future for all.

This is the great unfinished work of the American experiment, the constant struggle to live up to the noble ideals upon which our nation was founded. And though I may not live to see the day when the promise of the Declaration is fully realized, I can only hope that my own failings and regrets may serve as a spur to those who come after, a reminder of the work that still remains to be done.

For in the end, the true measure of our greatness as a people lies not in our wealth or our power, but in our willingness to confront the darkness within our own hearts, to stand up for what is right and just, even when the cost is high and the path is difficult.

And so, I offer these words as a humble plea for forgiveness, a testament to the terrible burden of a life lived in the shadow of hypocrisy and contradiction. May God have mercy on my soul, and may the nation I helped to found one day rise above the sins of its past, to become a true beacon of freedom and justice for all mankind.

# Chapter 9

# Hamlet

# The Slings and Arrows of Inaction

The weight of the crown hangs heavy upon my brow, a constant reminder of the duty I have failed to fulfill. I, Hamlet, Prince of Denmark, find myself trapped in a web of indecision, haunted by the ghost of my father and the knowledge of my uncle's treachery.

In the depths of my torment, I am consumed by a singular regret, a gnawing guilt that eats away at my very soul. The regret of hesitation, of the moments lost to doubt and inaction, the lives that could have been spared had I only found the courage to act.

I think back to that fateful night on the ramparts of Elsinore, when my father's spirit first revealed the truth of his murder. The betrayal of my uncle, the adultery of my mother, the poison that seeped into the very heart of our kingdom. In that moment, I knew what I had to do, the revenge I was called to exact.

But something stayed my hand, a paralyzing doubt that crept into my mind like a thief in the night. The question of certainty, the fear of damnation, the weight of the moral choice that lay before me. To kill a king, even a murderous one, was no small matter.

And so, I hesitated. I retreated into the labyrinth of my own thoughts, the endless cycle of contemplation and inaction. The play within the play, the madness I feigned, the love I spurned—all distractions from the true task at hand.

I think of the lives lost in the wake of my indecision. Polonius, slain by my own hand in a moment of impulsive rage. Ophelia, driven to madness and watery death by the cruelty of my rejection. Rosencrantz and Guildenstern, sacrificed as pawns in the game of kings.

And then, the final act, the culmination of my tragic tale. The duel with Laertes, the poisoned blade and chalice, the revelation of my uncle's treachery. In the end, it was not my hand that delivered justice, but the hand of fate, the collision of circumstance and consequence.

As I lie here, the life ebbing from my poisoned veins, I am haunted by the realization that my greatest enemy was not my uncle, but myself. My own weakness, my own inability to act, the paralyzing weight of my own thoughts.

I think of the kingdom I leave behind, the chaos and uncertainty that will follow in the wake of my death. The legacy of a prince who could not bear the burden of his own destiny, who let the rot of corruption fester until it consumed us all.

And yet, even in my final moments, I cling to a glimmer of hope, a faint possibility of redemption. The story of my life, the cautionary tale of the dangers of hesitation, may yet serve as a beacon to those who come after. A reminder that the path of righteousness, though difficult and fraught with peril, is the only path worth taking.

Let my regret be a lesson to all who bear the weight of power and responsibility. Let my failure be a call to action, a reminder that the greatest tragedy is not the fall of the mighty, but the silence of those who could have made a difference.

And so, I take my final bow, the curtain falling on the tragedy of Hamlet, Prince of Denmark. May my story endure, a testament to the human struggle, the battle between action and inaction, the search for meaning in a world of shadows and deceit.

# Chapter 10

# Macbeth

# The Dunsinane Dirge of Despair

The blood on my hands, once a symbol of my valor, now serves as a bitter reminder of the path I chose. I, Macbeth, Thane of Glamis and Cawdor, King of Scotland, sit upon a throne built on the bones of the innocent, haunted by the weight of my own ambition.

In the stillness of the night, I am visited by the specters of my regret, the ghosts of those whose lives I sacrificed on the altar of my own desire. The witches' prophecy, a seed planted in the fertile soil of my mind, grew into a twisted tree of obsession, its roots strangling the very essence of my humanity.

I think back to that fateful night, the dagger plunged into the heart of a sleeping king, a man who trusted me as a loyal subject and friend. The blood on my hands, the screams of my own conscience, drowned out by the intoxicating whispers of power and greatness.

In the pursuit of the crown, I lost sight of the true nature of greatness. I betrayed the very virtues that had once defined me—loyalty, honor, and compassion. I allowed myself to be consumed by the darkness within, the insidious voice that whispered promises of glory and immortality.

And what did I gain? A kingdom built on fear, a reign marked by paranoia and despair. The love and respect I once commanded, replaced by the hollow adulation of sycophants and the bitter resentment of those I had wronged.

I think of my beloved Lady Macbeth, the partner of my ambition and the sharer of my guilt. How I watched her unravel, consumed by the weight of our shared sin, her mind fracturing under the strain of a conscience she could not escape. Her death, a final testament to the destructive power of unchecked ambition.

And then, in the end, the realization of the futility of it all. The prophecy fulfilled, yet hollow and meaningless. The crown, a burden rather than a blessing, a symbol of the corruption that had eaten away at my very soul.

As I stand on the battlefield, facing the armies of those I have wronged, I am struck by the realization that my greatest regret is not the acts themselves, but the man I allowed myself to become. The tyrant, the murderer, the embodiment of the very evil I had once sworn to fight against.

In my final moments, I cling to the hope that my story may serve as a warning to those who follow, a cautionary tale of the dangers of unbridled ambition and the seductive lure of power. That my legacy may be not the blood-soaked pages of history, but the hard-earned wisdom of a man who lost himself in the pursuit of a hollow crown.

Let my regret be a reminder that true greatness lies not in the trappings of power, but in the integrity of one's soul. That the path of righteousness, though often difficult and fraught with sacrifice, is the only path worth taking.

And so, I embrace my fate, the final act in a tragedy of my own making. The curtain falls on the reign of Macbeth, a king who forgot the true meaning of kingship, a man who allowed his ambition to consume his humanity.

May my story endure as a testament to the destructive power of unchecked desire, and may those who come after learn from the mistakes of a man who dared to reach too high, and paid the ultimate price.

# Chapter 11

# King Lear

# The Madness of Majesty Unmoored

Howl, ye winds of regret, and bear witness to the tempest that rages within my shattered heart! I, Lear, once King of Britain, now stand as a testament to the folly of pride and the bitter fruit of misplaced trust.

In the twilight of my reign, I sought to divide my kingdom, to bestow upon my daughters the love and loyalty I so desperately craved. Yet, in my vanity, I failed to see the serpents that lurked behind fair faces and honeyed words. Goneril and Regan, the vipers I nurtured at my breast, turned their fangs upon me, stripping me of my power, my dignity, and the very essence of my being.

Oh, Cordelia, my sweet child, the one true light amidst the darkness! In my blindness, I cast you aside, banishing the only love that was pure and unyielding. How cruel the irony that it was your honesty, your refusal to flatter and deceive, that incurred my wrath and sealed our tragic fate.

Now, I wander the storm-ravaged heath, a king in name but a beggar in spirit. The elements rage around me, a physical manifestation of the anguish that tears at my soul. I am stripped bare, left to confront the harsh reality of my own hubris and the consequences of my actions.

As the storm within me reaches its crescendo, I am haunted by the specter of my own mortality. The weight of my regrets crashes upon me like the fury of the tempest, drowning out all hope of redemption. I am a man undone, a king reduced to a shadow of his former self, grasping at the tattered remnants of a life wasted on pride and folly.

And yet, in the depths of my despair, a flicker of clarity emerges, like a lone candle in the raging storm. I see now the true nature of love, the value of a heart that speaks with honesty and devotion. In my final moments, as I cradle the lifeless body of my beloved Cordelia, I am struck by the bitter realization that it was I who failed her, not she who failed me.

Let my story stand as a warning to those who would place their trust in false affections and shallow flattery. Let my fate be a reminder that the true measure of a king, of a father, lies not in the vastness of his domain, but in the depth of his love and the wisdom of his choices.

As the storm of my life reaches its end, I am left with nothing but the echoes of my own regret, the haunting refrain of "never, never, never, never, never." May the winds carry my tale across the ages, a testament to the destructive power of unchecked pride and the redemptive potential of true love and humility.

And so, I take my final bow, a once-mighty king laid low by the tempest of his own making. Let the heavens weep for Lear, and let the earth remember the hard-won wisdom of a man who learned, too late, the true nature of a shattered crown and a fractured soul.

# Chapter 12
# William Shakespeare
## The Bard's Lament

In the flickering candlelight of my study, I, William Shakespeare, find myself haunted by the ghosts of my own creation. As I dip my quill into the inkwell, the faces of Hamlet, Macbeth, and Lear swim before my eyes, their stories etched indelibly upon my soul.

I have spent my life spinning tales of love and loss, of triumph and tragedy, seeking to hold a mirror up to nature and reflect the depths of the human experience. And yet, as I look back upon my work, I cannot help but feel a sense of unease, a gnawing doubt that perhaps I have delved too deep into the darkest recesses of the heart.

In Hamlet, I gave voice to the anguish of a young prince torn between action and inaction, consumed by the weight of his own thoughts. I watched as he grappled with the specter of his father's ghost, the betrayal of his mother, and the cruel machinations of his uncle. And yet, even as I penned his soliloquies and charted his descent into madness, I couldn't help but wonder: did I do enough to illuminate the path of redemption, to offer a glimmer of hope amidst the darkness?

With Macbeth, I explored the seductive lure of ambition, the way in which the promise of power can corrupt even the noblest of souls. I watched as he and his lady plunged headlong into a maelstrom of blood and guilt, their hands forever stained by the sins of their own making. And yet, as I witnessed their fall, I couldn't help but question my own role in shaping their fate. Did I, in my zeal to craft a compelling narrative, neglect to offer a cautionary tale, a reminder of the perils of unbridled desire?

And then there is Lear, the once-great king brought low by his own hubris and the cruelty of his daughters. In him, I saw the fragility of the human condition, the way in which even the mightiest among us can be stripped bare by the tempests of fate. And yet, as I charted his descent into madness and despair, I couldn't help but wonder if I had done enough to underscore the redeeming power of love, the way in which even the darkest of storms can give way to a glimmer of grace.

As I sit here, surrounded by the labors of a lifetime, I am struck by the weight of my own responsibility. I have given life to these characters, breathed into them the joys and sorrows of the human experience. And yet, I cannot escape the feeling that I have somehow fallen short, that in my quest to plumb the depths of the soul, I have neglected to offer the balm of hope, the promise of redemption.

Perhaps it is the curse of the artist, to be forever haunted by the specters of one's own creation. To grapple with the knowledge that in holding a mirror up to nature, we cannot help but reflect the shadows as well as the light.

And yet, even in my moments of doubt, I cling to the belief that there is power in the telling of these tales, in the sharing of these human truths. For if my works have taught me anything, it is that we are all of us flawed and fallible creatures, stumbling through the mire of our own imperfections.

But it is in the crucible of these struggles that we find our humanity, that we come to know the true measure of our own strength. And it is through the telling of these stories that we may yet find the courage to confront our own demons, to seek the light amidst the darkness.

And so, I take up my pen once more, determined to give voice to the full spectrum of the human experience—the triumphs and the tragedies, the joys and the sorrows. For it is only in embracing the totality of who we are that we may hope to find the path to redemption, the way to make sense of the mystery of our own existence.

# Chapter 13

# Simón Bolívar

# The Unfulfilled Dream of Unity

In the fading light of my life, I, Simón Bolívar, Liberator of South America, find myself haunted by the specter of a dream unfulfilled. As I look upon the fractured continent I fought so hard to free, I cannot help but feel a profound sense of regret, a bitter acknowledgment that the unity and harmony I envisioned for my people remain elusive, even in the wake of our hard-won independence.

I think back to the early days of our struggle, when the fires of revolution first ignited in my heart. Born into privilege, I could have easily chosen a life of comfort and ease, but the cries of my oppressed compatriots echoed in my soul, and I knew that I could not rest until the chains of Spanish tyranny were broken.

For more than two decades, I led the charge against the colonial powers, rallying the people of Venezuela, Colombia, Ecuador,

Peru, and Bolivia to the banner of freedom. Through countless battles and insurmountable odds, we fought with the courage and tenacity of those who know that their cause is just, that the price of liberty is one worth paying.

And yet, even as we savored the sweet taste of victory, as we watched the flags of our newborn nations rise above the blood-stained soil, I could feel the seeds of discord and division taking root. The lofty ideals of pan-American unity, of a confederation of states bound by a common language, culture, and destiny, began to give way to the petty rivalries and ambitions of men.

I think of the countless hours I spent in the halls of government, trying to forge a lasting peace, to enshrine the principles of justice and equality in the very foundations of our new societies. But for every step forward, it seemed we took two back, as the forces of regionalism, factionalism, and self-interest conspired to tear us apart.

And now, as I lie on my deathbed, exiled and disillusioned, I cannot help but wonder if I could have done more, if there was some way I could have held the dream together. The continent I sought to unite is now a patchwork of nations, each one nursing its own grievances and grudges, each one more concerned with its own narrow interests than with the greater good of all.

But perhaps the greatest tragedy is not the fracturing of our political unity, but the betrayal of the social and economic justice for which we fought so hard. The lofty promises of equality and opportunity have given way to new forms of oppression, as the wealthy and powerful continue to profit at the expense of the poor and marginalized. The land reforms I championed, the redistribution of wealth and resources, have been largely undone, leaving the masses in a state of perpetual struggle and despair.

It is a bitter pill to swallow, the realization that the freedom we won on the battlefield has not translated into the kind of society I envisioned, one in which every man, woman, and child could live with dignity and hope. And yet, even in my darkest moments of doubt, I cannot help but cling to the belief that our struggle was not in vain, that the sacrifices we made will one day bear fruit in a more just and equitable world.

For the true legacy of our revolution, the enduring gift of the Liberator, is not to be found in the fleeting alliances of states or the shifting fortunes of politics, but in the unquenchable thirst for freedom and self-determination that burns in the hearts of all oppressed peoples. It is a fire that cannot be extinguished, a light that will continue to guide the way forward, even in the face of setbacks and adversity.

And so, as I take my final bow, as the curtain falls on the turbulent drama of my life, I can only hope that the dream of unity and justice will live on, that future generations will take up the mantle of our struggle and carry it forward to its ultimate fulfillment. For though the road may be long and the challenges great, I know that the spirit of liberation that animated our cause will never die, that the quest for a better world is one that will forever endure.

# Chapter 14

# Napoleon Bonaparte

## The Specter of Moscow

The flames of the hearth dance before my eyes, casting flickering shadows across the walls of my exile. The chill of the Atlantic seeps into my bones, a constant reminder of how far I have fallen. But it is not the cold that haunts me, nor the chains that bind me to this rock. It is the memory of a single decision, a moment that sealed my fate and changed the course of history.

Moscow. The very name is a blade in my heart, a wound that will not heal. I close my eyes and I am back on that fateful battlefield, the smoke of a thousand fires obscuring the horizon. The grand city, the jewel of the Russian Empire, laid to waste by the flames of war.

I had marched my armies across the continent, certain of my invincibility, convinced that nothing could stand in the way of my destiny. But I had not reckoned with the resilience of the Russian spirit, the willingness of a people to sacrifice everything in defense of their homeland.

The road to Moscow was a trail of blood and ashes, littered with the bodies of my soldiers. The bitter cold, the endless steppes, the scorched earth tactics of the enemy—all conspired to sap the strength from my men, to turn a glorious campaign into a nightmare of suffering and despair.

And yet, even as I stood in the ruins of the Kremlin, the weight of my hubris bearing down upon me, I could not bring myself to admit defeat. I clung to the belief that I could salvage something from this disaster, that I could yet snatch victory from the jaws of defeat.

But it was not to be. The long retreat, the endless miles of frozen wasteland, the harrying attacks of the Cossacks—all took their toll. My once mighty army, the instrument of my will, reduced to a ragged band of survivors, stumbling through the snow in a desperate bid for survival.

The specter of Moscow haunts me still, a reminder of the fragility of power, the price of overreach. In my arrogance, I had believed myself invincible, a conqueror destined to reshape the world in my image. But the ruins of the Kremlin, the ashes of my ambitions, serve as a bitter testament to the folly of my pride.

I am Napoleon, Emperor of the French, master of Europe. But in the end, I was undone by my own hubris, by the belief that I could bend the world to my will through sheer force of arms.

The lesson of Moscow, the truth that I learned too late, is that there are limits to power, that even the greatest of men can be brought low by the tides of history. That in war, as in life, the only true victory is the one that is earned through humility, through the recognition of one's own limitations.

As I sit here in exile, the waves of the Atlantic crashing against the rocks, I am haunted by the ghosts of the past, by the faces of the men who followed me to their doom. And I know that I will carry the burden of their sacrifice, the weight of my own failure, for the rest of my days.

For I am Napoleon, the once and future Emperor, the man who dared to challenge the world. And in the end, it was the world that proved the victor, that showed me the price of my own hubris.

But even in defeat, I remain unbowed, a testament to the indomitable spirit of France, to the enduring power of the human will. And though the specter of Moscow may haunt me still, I know that my legacy will endure, that the name of Napoleon will echo through the ages, a symbol of the heights to which a man may climb, and the depths to which he may fall.

# Chapter 15

# Lord Cardigan

# The Shadow of the Valley

The clatter of hooves has long since faded, replaced by the relentless ticking of the grandfather clock in the hall. It's a mocking reminder of time, of moments that can never be undone, of a decision that echoes through the desolate chambers of my soul.

I sit in my study, the once vibrant colors of the room muted by the encroaching darkness. My medals gleam dully in the dim light, hollow symbols of a glory stained with blood.

The image of that fateful day at Balaclava haunts me, a ghastly spectacle seared into my memory. The Light Brigade, my men, charging valiantly into the valley of death, their sabers flashing in the afternoon sun. A magnificent sight, yet a horrifying one.

The roar of the cannons, the screams of the wounded, the sickening thud of bodies hitting the ground. It was a massacre, a senseless sacrifice of brave men sent to their doom by a muddled order.

And I, Lord Cardigan, led them into that inferno. The weight of their lives rests heavy on my conscience, a burden that grows heavier with each passing day.

They say I was a proud man, arrogant, even. Perhaps it's true. But beneath the veneer of confidence, there was always a flicker of doubt, a gnawing insecurity that drove me to seek validation on the battlefield.

In that moment, as I watched my men ride to their deaths, the facade crumbled. All that remained was the stark realization of my folly, the bitter taste of regret.

I had been given a command, a senseless one, and I obeyed without question. In my blind obedience, I condemned hundreds of men to a brutal and unnecessary end.

The cheers of victory turned to whispers of condemnation. The accolades of the past were drowned out by the cries of the widows and orphans. I became a pariah, a symbol of the futility of war, a cautionary tale of blind obedience.

I try to find solace in the fact that I too charged into the valley, that I faced the same dangers as my men. But it is a hollow comfort. I survived, while they perished. I am left to bear the guilt, the shame, the agonizing knowledge that I could have done more to protect them.

The ticking of the clock grows louder, each tick a hammer blow to my soul. The darkness closes in, and the faces of the fallen rise before me, their eyes accusing, their voices echoing in the desolate chambers of my heart.

I am a broken man, haunted by the ghosts of Balaclava. The Charge of the Light Brigade will forever be my legacy, a monument to my hubris and my failure as a leader. And in the quiet of the night, as the shadows lengthen and the echoes of the past grow louder, I am left to grapple with the bitter truth: that the greatest regret of my life is the one that can never be undone.

# Chapter 16

# Sarah Graves

## The Bitter Taste of Survival

In the solitude of my final days, as the warmth of the California sun falls upon my weathered face, I, Sarah Graves, find myself haunted by the ghosts of that fateful winter, the memories of the Donner Party forever seared into my soul. The decisions we made, the unspeakable acts we committed in the name of survival—these are the burdens I have carried with me through the long years of my life, the bitter price of living to tell our tale.

I think back to the early days of our journey, when the promise of a new life in the West filled our hearts with hope and anticipation. We were a band of pioneers, brave souls who had left behind the comfort and security of civilization to seek our fortunes in the untamed wilderness. Little did we know then the horrors that awaited us, the depths of despair and depravity to which we would sink in the face of unimaginable adversity.

As the delays and setbacks mounted, as the winter snows began to fall and the passes through the mountains grew treacherous, I watched as the bonds of our makeshift community began to fray. Tempers flared, resentments simmered, and the once-unbreakable ties of friendship and family gave way to a grim calculus of survival.

And then came the storm, the relentless blizzard that trapped us in that godforsaken camp by the lake, our supplies dwindling and our hopes of rescue fading with each passing day. It was there, in the frozen hell of Truckee Lake, that we faced the ultimate test of our humanity, the unthinkable choice between death and damnation.

I remember the first time the whispers began, the furtive glances and hushed conversations that hinted at the unspeakable. The thought of consuming the flesh of our fallen companions, of violating the most sacred taboos of civilized society in order to cling to life—it was a horror beyond imagining, a nightmare made real by the cruel indifference of nature.

And yet, as the days turned to weeks and the specter of starvation loomed ever closer, I found myself grappling with the same terrible dilemma that haunted us all. Could I watch my own child waste away before my eyes, knowing that a few morsels of human flesh might sustain her for another day? Could I live with myself if I partook of that forbidden sustenance, if I crossed the line that separated man from beast in the name of survival?

In the end, I made my choice, as we all did in that frozen wasteland. With trembling hands and a heart heavy with grief, I joined in the grim ritual of cannibalism, the last resort of the desperate and the damned. And though the meat sustained our bodies, it could not nourish our souls, could not erase the stain of guilt and shame that would mark us for the rest of our lives.

Even now, decades later, the memory of those dark days haunts my every waking moment. The faces of the dead, the anguished cries of the dying, the bitter taste of human flesh upon my tongue - these are the ghosts that will follow me to my grave, the price I paid for my own survival.

And yet, even in the depths of my regret, I cannot help but wonder if I would make the same choice again, if faced with the same impossible circumstances. For in the end, the will to live is a force more powerful than any moral code, any civilized notion of right and wrong. When the very essence of our humanity is stripped away by the pitiless hand of fate, what are we left with but the primal instinct to endure, to cling to existence at any cost?

Perhaps that is the true legacy of the Donner Party, the grim lesson that echoes through the annals of history. That in the face of unimaginable hardship and suffering, the human spirit is capable of both extraordinary resilience and unfathomable darkness. That the line between survival and savagery is a thin and fragile one, easily crossed in the heat of desperation.

As I look back on that fateful winter, on the choices we made and the horrors we endured, I am filled with a profound sense of sorrow and regret. For the innocence lost, for the lives shattered, for the scars that will never fully heal. But I am also filled with a strange and solemn pride, a recognition of the incredible strength and determination that carried us through the worst of human ordeals.

For in the end, we did what we had to do to survive, to claw our way back from the brink of oblivion and emerge, forever changed, into the light of a new day. And though the memory of that dark chapter will haunt me to the end of my days, I know that it is also a testament to the indomitable power of the human will, the fierce and unrelenting force that drives us to endure, to persevere, to live on in the face of even the most impossible odds.

So let my story stand as a reminder of the fragility of our shared humanity, of the delicate balance between civilization and savagery that we all must navigate in the face of adversity. And let it also serve as a tribute to the resilience of the human spirit, to the unbreakable bonds of love and sacrifice that can carry us through even the darkest of nights.

For ultimately, the bitter taste of survival is a small price to pay for the chance to bear witness, to carry the memory of those we lost and the lessons we learned into the uncertain future that lies ahead. And though the ghosts of Truckee Lake may never truly leave me, I know that they are also a part of me now, a reminder of the depths of human experience and the indomitable will to live that defines us all.

# Chapter 17

# George Armstrong Custer

## The Last Stand of Pride

In the eternal realm of reflection, where the echoes of battle have long since faded, I, Lieutenant Colonel George Armstrong Custer, find myself haunted by the specter of my own hubris. The golden locks that once crowned my head, now matted with the blood of my own folly, serve as a bitter reminder of the pride that led me to my doom on the banks of the Little Bighorn.

I recall the days leading up to that fateful battle, the sense of invincibility that coursed through my veins as I led my troops across the vast expanses of the American West. We were the 7th Cavalry, the pride of the U.S. Army, and I was their commander, a rising star in the military firmament. I had made a name for myself in the Civil War, my daring exploits and tactical brilliance earning me the admiration of my superiors and the adulation of the public.

But as we rode deeper into the untamed wilderness of Montana Territory, chasing the elusive shadows of the Lakota and Cheyenne warriors, I began to feel the weight of my own legend bearing down upon me. The newspapers back East had painted me as a hero, a savior of the frontier, and I could not bear the thought of failing to live up to that image. I was determined to win a decisive victory against the Native American forces, to crush their resistance once and for all and secure my place in the annals of history.

In my arrogance, I made the fateful decision to divide my regiment, sending one detachment to scout ahead while I led the main force in pursuit of the enemy. I was convinced that the warriors we faced were no match for the superior firepower and discipline of my troops, that we could easily overwhelm them with a swift and bold attack.

But as we crested the ridge above the Little Bighorn River and saw the sprawling encampment of the Lakota and Cheyenne below, I began to realize the depth of my miscalculation. The valley was teeming with thousands of warriors, far more than our intelligence had suggested, and they were ready for battle. In that moment, I felt the first stirrings of doubt, the sickening realization that I had led my men into a trap from which there would be no escape.

What followed was a maelstrom of blood and chaos, a desperate fight for survival against overwhelming odds. I watched as my men were cut down one by one, their screams of agony mingling with the war cries of the advancing warriors. And in the midst of that horror, as the bullets tore through the air and the arrows found their marks, I could not escape the brutal truth of my own responsibility.

I had underestimated my enemy, had failed to heed the warnings of my scouts and the wisdom of my subordinates. In my quest for glory and recognition, I had driven my command to the brink of annihilation, had sacrificed the lives of brave men on the altar of my own vanity. And now, as the shadows grew long and the last of my soldiers fell around me, I knew that I would forever be remembered not as a hero, but as a cautionary tale of the perils of blind ambition.

In the years since my death on that blood-soaked battlefield, as the myth of "Custer's Last Stand" has taken root in the American imagination, I have been forced to confront the bitter irony of my own legacy. The very qualities that had once been celebrated as the hallmarks of my leadership—my boldness, my daring, my unwavering confidence in the face of the enemy—had become the seeds of my own destruction, the fatal flaws that led me to my doom.

And yet, even as I grapple with the weight of my own failures, I cannot help but feel a sense of sorrow for the larger tragedy that my story represents. For in the end, the Battle of the Little Bighorn was not just a clash of arms, but a collision of cultures, a brutal reckoning between the relentless push of manifest destiny and the desperate struggle of indigenous peoples to preserve their way of life.

I see now the arrogance and the folly of the belief that one nation, one way of life, could lay claim to an entire continent, that the march of progress could justify the destruction of whole societies and the dispossession of entire peoples. And I am haunted by the realization that my own actions, my own misguided sense of duty and destiny, played a part in that larger tragedy.

The Battle of the Little Bighorn stands as a stark reminder of the complex and often brutal realities of history. The grand narratives of nations frequently obscure the human costs of conquest and conflict, and my own story serves as a potent example of this.

In the echoes of that distant battle, in the mingled blood of the fallen on both sides, there are lessons to be learned about the dangers of unchecked ambition and the perils of cultural myopia. Grappling with these painful realities is a necessary step in understanding our shared history and the ways in which it continues to shape our world today.

# Chapter 18

# Sitting Bull

# The Wounds of a Warrior's Soul

In the twilight of my days, as I look upon the once-vast expanse of our ancestral lands, now diminished and confined, I, Sitting Bull, chief and holy man of the Hunkpapa Lakota, feel the weight of a life marked by struggle and loss. The scars on my body tell the story of a warrior who fought fiercely to protect his people, but it is the wounds of my spirit that whisper the tale of my deepest regrets.

I think back to the days of my youth, when the plains stretched out before us like an endless sea of grass, and the buffalo roamed in numbers beyond counting. We lived as our ancestors had, in harmony with the land and the spirits that guided our every step. But even then, I could see the shadows on the horizon, the gathering storm of change that threatened to engulf us all.

As the years passed and the encroachment of the white man grew ever more relentless, I found myself thrust into the role of a leader, a voice for my people in the face of an enemy that sought to strip us of our land, our way of life, and our very identity. I fought with all the strength and cunning of a warrior, leading my people in battle against the soldiers who would see us destroyed.

But even as I claimed victories on the battlefield, I could not shake the sense that we were fighting a losing war. The white man's numbers were too great, their weapons too powerful, and their hunger for our land too insatiable. I watched as our once-vast territory was whittled away by treaties and broken promises, as our people were forced onto ever-smaller reservations, our children taken from us to be "civilized" in the white man's schools.

And yet, even in the face of these overwhelming odds, I clung to the belief that we could find a way to preserve our way of life, to hold fast to the traditions and beliefs that had sustained us for generations. I sought to unite the tribes, to form a coalition that could stand against the tide of westward expansion and protect what was rightfully ours.

But in my zeal to resist, I fear that I may have led my people down a path of even greater suffering—a path paved with the bones of our own. The wars we fought, the lives we lost—these are burdens that weigh heavily on my soul. I think of the young men who fell in battle, their bodies left to rot on the plains, their families left to mourn their loss. I think of the women and children who starved and sickened in the squalor of the reservations, the once-proud Lakota reduced to a life of poverty and despair.

I am haunted by the whispers of what might have been, the paths left untraveled. Perhaps there was another way, a road to peace and coexistence that I failed to see. The voices of those who sought compromise, who dared to dream of a world where the Lakota and the white man could walk side by side—I silenced them in my pride and my rage. I dismissed their voices, seeing only weakness and capitulation in their words. I believed that the only way to protect our people was through strength and resistance, that to compromise was to surrender our very soul.

Now, as the sun sets on my life, I am left to grapple with the bitter fruit of my own choices, the knowledge that for all my strength and all my wisdom, I could not save my people from the fate that awaited us. The ghost dance, the sacred ritual that I believed would usher in a new era of hope and renewal, instead brought only more pain and suffering, as the soldiers descended upon our camps with guns blazing.

In the final reckoning, I was left to watch as my people were scattered to the winds, our way of life all but extinguished, our once-great nation reduced to a shadow of its former self. And though I know that I fought with all the courage and conviction of a true warrior, I cannot escape the sense that I failed them, that I could not find a way to lead them to a better future.

With a heavy heart, I offer these words as a testament to the weight of my regrets, the sorrows that I will carry with me into the great beyond. To the Lakota, to all the indigenous peoples of this land, I offer my apologies for the failures of leadership that left us broken and diminished. And to the generations yet unborn, I offer this hard-earned truth: never forget the sacrifices of those who came before, and never let the fires of resistance and pride blind you to the wisdom of peace and understanding.

For it is not the victories we claim or the foes we vanquish that measure our worth, but the grace and humanity we embody in the face of adversity. Though my journey was stained with blood and tears, I hold fast to the hope that those who follow will chart a new course, one that honors our past while embracing the promise of tomorrow.

May the Great Spirit grant us the courage and the vision to find that path, and may the wounds of my own soul serve as a reminder of the price we pay when we let our fears and our anger consume us. For only by learning from the mistakes of the past can we hope to build a future that is worthy of our children and our children's children, a world in which the Lakota and all the peoples of this earth can live in peace, prosperity, and enduring hope.

# Chapter 19

# Karl Marx

## The Dialectic of Disillusionment

As I sit in the fading light of my study, the weight of history bearing down upon my shoulders, I, Karl Marx, find myself haunted by the specter of a revolution gone astray, a vision of liberation twisted into a nightmare of oppression and suffering.

The pages of my life's work, the ink still wet with the fervor of my convictions, lie scattered before me, a testament to the power of ideas to shape the course of human events. And yet, as I reflect on the legacy of my thoughts, the unintended consequences of my call to arms, I cannot help but feel a profound sense of regret and responsibility.

I think back to the early days of my intellectual journey, when the injustices of the capitalist system first stirred the fires of rebellion in my heart. The plight of the working class, the alienation and exploitation of the proletariat, the corrupt foundations of bourgeois society—these were the wrongs I sought to right, the chains I hoped to break through the force of revolutionary fervor.

And yet, as I watch the unfolding of the 20th century, the rise of totalitarian regimes that claim the mantle of Marxism, I am filled with a growing sense of unease and disillusionment. The Soviet Union, China, Cambodia—these were not the classless utopias I envisioned, but rather twisted perversions of my ideas, brutal dictatorships that trampled upon the very freedoms and dignities I held dear.

I think of the millions of lives lost, the families torn apart, the hopes and dreams crushed beneath the boot of oppression. The gulags and the killing fields, the censorship and the thought police—these were not the fruits of the revolution I had imagined, but rather the bitter harvest of a dream betrayed.

And then there is the question of economic transformation, the promise of a world free from the shackles of capitalist exploitation. But as I witness the stagnation and scarcity, the inefficiencies and absurdities of centrally planned economies, I am forced to confront the limitations of my own theories, the hubris of my belief in the infallible march of history.

Perhaps, in my zeal to overthrow the old order, I underestimated the resilience of the human spirit, the desire for individual agency and self-determination. Perhaps I failed to fully grasp the complexities of economic systems, the delicate balance between incentives and equity, between freedom and security.

And then there is the matter of my own legacy, the way in which my name and my ideas have been twisted and distorted to serve the ends of tyrants and demagogues. The very word "Marxism" has become a cudgel, a shorthand for all that is radical and threatening, a bogeyman invoked to stifle dissent and justify oppression.

I think of the countless intellectual and political movements that have claimed me as their patron saint, from the revolutionary vanguards of the early 20th century to the academic theorists of the modern day. And yet, how many of them have truly grappled with the subtleties of my thought, the nuances of my critique? How many have used my name as a mask for their own agendas, a convenient label to lend legitimacy to their own desires for power and control?

As I reflect on the weight of my regrets, the burden of my intellectual legacy, I cannot help but feel a profound sense of sorrow and responsibility. The dream of a world free from oppression and exploitation, a society of true equality and solidarity—this was the vision that animated my life's work, the fire that burned in my soul until the very end.

But now, as I survey the wreckage of the 20th century, the shattered hopes and the broken lives, I am forced to confront the painful truth that my ideas, for all their noble intentions, have been wielded as weapons of destruction and domination.

And yet, even in the depths of my despair, I cannot entirely abandon the conviction that a better world is possible, that the struggle for justice and liberation must continue. The errors and the excesses of the past, the betrayals and the distortions—these are not the final word on the human story, but rather the birth pangs of a new era, a world yet to be born.

Perhaps, in the end, my true legacy will not be the regimes and the movements that have claimed my name, but rather the countless individuals who have been inspired by my critique, who have taken up the banner of resistance and solidarity in the face of oppression and injustice.

For the true meaning of Marxism, the beating heart of my life's work, lies not in the dogmas and the dictatorships, but in the eternal struggle for human dignity and liberation, the unwavering belief in the power of the people to shape their own destiny.

And so, even as I grapple with the weight of my own mistakes and the unintended consequences of my ideas, I cling to the hope that the spirit of my thought, the essence of my critique, will endure long after the distortions and the betrayals have faded into history.

For in the final analysis, the true measure of a life, of a philosophy, lies not in the accolades of the present or the monuments of the past, but in the enduring power of its vision to inspire and to transform, to light the way forward for generations yet to come.

And it is in this spirit that I offer my own story, my own grappling with the weight of history, as a testament to the unending struggle for a world of true freedom and equality, a world in which the specter of oppression and exploitation will at last be laid to rest, and the full potential of the human spirit will at last be realized.

# Chapter 20

# Sigmund Freud

## The Psychoanalysis of Regret

In the twilight of my life, as I sit in the quiet of my study, surrounded by the volumes that bear witness to a lifetime of inquiry into the labyrinthine depths of the human mind, I, Sigmund Freud, find myself confronted by a most peculiar and persistent visitor: the specter of my own regrets.

As the father of psychoanalysis, I have devoted my years to the exploration of the hidden realms of the psyche, to the excavation of the buried traumas and desires that shape the contours of our conscious experience. And yet, as I turn my gaze inward, I cannot help but feel a sense of unease, a gnawing awareness that perhaps my own mind is not immune to the repressed conflicts and unresolved longings that I have so assiduously studied in others.

I think back to the early days of my career, when the insights of psychoanalysis first began to take shape in my thoughts. I was consumed by a passionate desire to unravel the mysteries of the mind, to lay bare the secret springs of human behavior. And in my zeal to construct a comprehensive theory of the psyche, I found myself drawn again and again to the central role of sexual desire, to the way in which our infantile erotic wishes and fears continue to exert a profound influence on our adult lives.

But as my ideas gained currency and my reputation grew, I began to feel a creeping sense of unease, a worry that perhaps my emphasis on sexuality had been too narrow, too reductive. I watched as my theories were sensationalized and misunderstood, as they became a source of scandal and ridicule in the popular press. And I could not help but wonder if, in my single-minded pursuit of a unified theory of the mind, I had neglected other equally important aspects of human experience.

As I reflect on this regret, I cannot help but see in it the echoes of my own unresolved infantile conflicts. Perhaps my fixation on sexual theories was itself a manifestation of my own repressed desires, a projection of my own unconscious wishes onto the blank screen of scientific inquiry. Perhaps, in my eagerness to assert the primacy of the libido, I was attempting to master my own unruly impulses, to impose order and meaning on the chaos of my own inner world.

And then there was my relationship with Carl Jung, my once-beloved disciple and confidant, whose brilliant mind and expansive vision had seemed to promise a new era of psychoanalytic discovery. But as our theoretical differences began to mount, as Jung's ideas veered ever further from the orthodoxy of my own, I found myself consumed by a sense of betrayal and resentment. The bitter rift that followed was a wound that never fully healed, a loss that I still feel keenly in the solitude of my final years.

As I contemplate this regret, I am reminded of the classic struggle between father and son, the oedipal drama that lies at the heart of so much human conflict. Perhaps my inability to find a way to reconcile with Jung, to forge a new synthesis of our ideas, was rooted in my own unresolved ambivalence towards the figure of the father, towards the authority and tradition that he represents. Perhaps, in my need to assert my own intellectual dominance, I had sacrificed the possibility of a more collaborative and generative partnership.

But of all my regrets, perhaps the one that weighs most heavily on my heart is the realization that, for all the profound insights and transformative potential of psychoanalysis, its therapeutic efficacy has often been called into question. I think of the countless patients who have passed through my consulting room over the years, the tortured souls who have laid bare their deepest fears and desires in the hope of finding relief and healing. And I cannot escape the nagging doubt that, in many cases, my method may have fallen short, may have offered only a partial or temporary respite from the suffering of the human condition.

As I analyze this regret, I am struck by the way in which it reflects my own deep-seated anxieties and insecurities, my own fear of failure and inadequacy. Perhaps my stubborn adherence to the tenets of psychoanalysis, my reluctance to adapt or evolve my approach in the face of new evidence and challenges, was itself a kind of defense mechanism, a way of clinging to the familiar and the safe in the face of an uncertain and ever-changing world.

And yet, even as I grapple with these regrets, these painful reminders of my own fallibility and limitations, I cannot help but feel a sense of pride and gratitude for the journey that has been my life's work. For in the end, the true value of psychoanalysis lies not in its ability to provide easy answers or definitive cures, but in its unwavering commitment to the exploration of the human soul, to the recognition of the depth and complexity of the inner world that we all inhabit.

And so, as I sit here in the gathering dusk, the shadows of my study lengthening around me, I offer these reflections not as a final verdict on my legacy, but as an invitation to those who come after me to continue the work that I have begun. To approach the study of the mind with the same passion and curiosity, the same willingness to confront the difficult truths and uncomfortable realities that lie at the heart of the human experience.

For it is only by embracing the full complexity of our psychic lives, by facing our deepest fears and desires with honesty and compassion, that we can hope to find the healing and the wholeness that we all seek. And it is in this ongoing process of self-discovery and self-acceptance that the true power of psychoanalysis resides, the transformative potential that has been my life's great calling and my most enduring contribution to the world.

# Chapter 21

# Alfred Dreyfus

## The Scars of Injustice

In the quiet of my study, far from the clamor of Paris streets and the echoes of military courts, I, Alfred Dreyfus, find myself haunted by the ghosts of a past that refuses to fade. The weight of years spent on Devil's Island still presses upon my shoulders, a burden that no exoneration can fully lift.

I close my eyes and I am there again, on that fateful day in 1894, standing before my fellow officers as they stripped me of my rank. The sound of my sword being broken, the buttons torn from my uniform—these are the sounds that still ring in my ears, drowning out the vindication that came too late.

How naive I was then, believing that my innocence would be my shield, that the truth would inevitably triumph. I had faith in the system, in the honor of the French military, in the justice of my beloved country. That faith was shattered, piece by piece, with every passing day of my imprisonment.

Devil's Island. The very name sends a chill through my body. The isolation, the heat, the constant battling against disease and despair—these were my companions for years. But perhaps the greatest torment was the knowledge that somewhere, the real traitor walked free, while I, an innocent man, bore the punishment for his crimes.

I think of my family, of my dear Lucie and our children, forced to bear the shame and ostracism that came with my conviction. The years of separation, the milestones missed, the precious moments of life that can never be reclaimed—these are the true casualties of injustice.

And yet, even as I grapple with the bitterness of those lost years, I find myself haunted by a deeper, more insidious regret. For in the aftermath of my ordeal, as the truth of my innocence came to light and the scandal of the affair rocked France to its core, I realized that my personal tragedy had exposed something far more sinister—the deep-seated anti-Semitism that lurked beneath the surface of French society.

I had always considered myself a Frenchman first, a patriot devoted to my country. But the affair stripped away that illusion, forcing me to confront the harsh reality that in the eyes of many, I would always be an outsider, a Jew first and a Frenchman second.

This realization has left me with a profound sense of disillusionment, a lingering doubt about the very foundations of the society I once believed in so fervently. I find myself questioning everything—the ideals of liberty, equality, and fraternity that France holds so dear, the notion of justice that I once thought inviolable.

Perhaps my greatest regret is that I cannot simply put this all behind me, that I cannot find it in my heart to forgive and forget. The scars run too deep, the memories too painful. Even now, years after my exoneration and reinstatement, I feel the weight of those years on Devil's Island, the sting of betrayal, the bitter taste of injustice.

And yet, I cannot help but wonder if my suffering has served some greater purpose. The Dreyfus Affair, as they call it now, has forced France to confront its demons, to grapple with the anti-Semitism and corruption that had festered for too long. Perhaps, in some small way, my ordeal has contributed to a more just and equitable society.

But at what cost? As I sit here, surrounded by the trappings of my restored life, I am left to ponder the price of justice delayed, the toll that injustice takes not just on the individual, but on the very fabric of society.

I am a free man now, my name cleared, my rank restored. But freedom, I have learned, is a complex thing. For while my body is no longer confined to that desolate island, my mind remains a prisoner of the past, forever grappling with the legacy of an injustice that can never truly be undone.

May my story serve as a warning to future generations, a reminder of the fragility of justice and the terrible consequences of prejudice and blind nationalism. For only by confronting the darkest chapters of our history can we hope to build a future worthy of the ideals we claim to hold dear.

# Chapter 22

# Georg Cantor

## The Burden of Unveiling Infinity's Paradox

As I sit in the quiet of my study, surrounded by the symbols and equations that have consumed my life's work, I, Georg Cantor, find myself haunted by a gnawing sense of unease. The very foundations of mathematics, once thought to be unshakable, now seem to tremble beneath the weight of the revelations I have unleashed upon the world.

My exploration of the infinite, the audacious notion that there are different sizes of infinity, has opened a Pandora's box of paradoxes and contradictions. The implications of my work stretch far beyond the realm of pure mathematics, casting doubt upon the very nature of reality and our place within it.

I think back to the moment when I first grasped the enormity of my discovery, the realization that the infinity of the natural numbers was but a mere speck compared to the vast, untamed wilderness of the continuum. The sheer audacity of this idea, the hubris of a mere mortal daring to quantify the unquantifiable, to compare the incomparable—it took my breath away.

But as the true significance of my work began to dawn on me, I couldn't help but feel a creeping sense of dread. The very concept of infinity, once a source of wonder and inspiration, now seemed to mock the limits of human understanding, to challenge the foundations upon which our knowledge of the world was built.

I think of the great thinkers of the past, the philosophers and theologians who sought to find meaning and purpose in the infinite. From Aristotle to Aquinas, the notion of an infinite God, an unbounded and unknowable creator, had been a cornerstone of religious thought. But my work, with its hierarchy of infinities and its paradoxical implications, seemed to call into question the very coherence of such a concept.

If there are multiple infinities, each one greater than the last, then what does it mean to speak of an infinite God? Is the divine merely one infinity among many, or does it transcend even the most unimaginable reaches of Cantor's paradise? These are the questions that haunt me, the doubts that gnaw at the edges of my certainty.

And then there are the scientific implications of my work, the ways in which it seems to undermine the very principles upon which our understanding of the physical world is built. If the continuum is not a single, unbroken whole, but rather a fractal landscape of infinities within infinities, then what does that mean for the smooth, continuous fabric of space and time that we take for granted?

I think of the great edifice of classical physics, the clockwork universe of Newton and Laplace, and I cannot help but wonder if my work has sown the seeds of its undoing. The notion of a deterministic, predictable cosmos seems to crumble in the face of the chaotic infinities that my theory has unleashed.

And so, I find myself torn between the thrill of discovery and the weight of responsibility. The mathematician in me revels in the beauty and elegance of the ideas I have brought to light, the sheer intellectual audacity of peering into the very heart of the infinite. But the human in me, the mortal creature of flesh and blood, cannot help but tremble at the implications of what I have wrought.

In my darker moments, I wonder if I have unleashed a monster, a mathematical demon that will forever haunt the dreams of those who seek to understand the nature of reality. The burden of this knowledge, the weight of the truths that I have uncovered, feels at times too heavy to bear.

But even in the midst of my doubts and fears, I cannot bring myself to regret the path I have chosen. For the pursuit of truth, no matter how unsettling or disquieting, is the highest calling of the mathematician, the noblest purpose to which a mind can be dedicated.

And so, I will continue to follow the numbers wherever they may lead, to plumb the depths of the infinite and the infinitesimal, to seek out the patterns and the structures that lie hidden beneath the surface of reality. It is not the destination that matters, but the journey itself, the ever-unfolding quest for knowledge and understanding that drives us forward into the unknown.

Let the philosophers and the theologians grapple with the implications of my work, let the scientists and the physicists reckon with the new realities that I have uncovered. For me, there is only the beauty of the mathematics, the pure, unadulterated joy of discovery that has been my constant companion throughout this long and winding road.

And though the burden of my knowledge may weigh heavily upon me, though the paradoxes and the contradictions may at times seem insurmountable, I will press on, secure in the knowledge that the truth, no matter how elusive or unsettling, is always worth pursuing.

It is my hope that the legacy of Georg Cantor will not be measured in the accolades or the accomplishments, but in the enduring impact of the ideas that I have set in motion, the ripples of thought and inspiration that will continue to spread outward, to shape and transform the very fabric of our understanding, long after I am gone.

# Chapter 23

# Adam

# The Bitter Fruit of Knowledge

In the twilight of my days, as I walk amidst the thorns and thistles of the world beyond Eden, I, Adam, the first man, fashioned from dust by the hand of the Almighty, find myself consumed by the weight of a regret that has haunted me since that fateful day in the Garden.

The Tree of Knowledge, its fruit gleaming in the sun like drops of crimson dew, the promise of wisdom and understanding hanging tantalizingly from its branches. How could I have known the cost of such knowledge, the terrible price that would be exacted for a single taste of that forbidden fruit?

Eve, my companion, my soul's other half, held out the fruit to me, her eyes bright with the hunger for enlightenment. The serpent's words echoed in my mind, the seductive whisper of the deceiver promising godlike understanding and the shattering of all limits. In that moment, my love for her, my desire to share in her fate, overcame the warning that echoed in my heart.

I took the fruit and raised it to my lips, the skin yielding beneath my teeth like the tender flesh of a newborn. The knowledge, the awareness of good and evil, flooded through me like a torrent of fire, searing away the innocence and trust that had once enveloped us like a garment of light.

In that instant, everything changed. The veil of blissful ignorance was torn asunder, and we saw ourselves as we truly were—naked and ashamed, our disobedience laid bare before the eyes of our Creator. The voice of God, once a melody of love and fellowship, now thundered with the wrath of judgment, the terrible price of our betrayal.

Banished from Eden, cast out into a world of toil and suffering, we felt the full weight of our transgression. The ground, once soft and yielding beneath our feet, now resisted our every step, the thorns and thistles a constant reminder of the paradise we had lost. The very creation that had once sung with joy at our presence now groaned in travail, the pains of childbirth a searing echo of our own agony.

But it was not just the physical hardships that tormented me, the sweat of my brow and the ache of my limbs as I tilled the unyielding earth. No, the true anguish lay in the knowledge of what I had lost, the realization of the innocence and communion that had been torn away by my own hand.

The memory of walking with God in the cool of the evening, His presence a balm to my soul, now burned like a brand of sorrow upon my heart. The trust and unity that had once flowed between myself and Eve, the perfect partners in a dance of love and obedience, had been shattered by recrimination and blame.

And then there was the terrible knowledge of my own legacy, the curse that I had brought upon all of my descendants. The sin that had found its roots in my own heart would now spread like a vile weed through all the generations of humanity, a bitter harvest of death and separation from the One who had formed us from the dust.

How often have I lain awake in the dark of night, the weight of that guilt pressing upon my chest like a mountain of despair? How many tears have I shed, the salt of my own sorrow mingling with the sweat of my labor, as I struggled to comprehend the magnitude of what had been lost?

And yet, even in the depths of my anguish, there was a glimmer of hope, a whisper of promise that echoed through the ages. The words of the Almighty to the serpent, that ancient deceiver, hinting at a future redemption, a seed of the woman who would one day crush the head of the enemy and restore what had been lost.

It is this hope that sustains me now, as the shadows of death lengthen and the years of my sojourn draw to a close. The knowledge that my story, the tale of my own tragic fall, is but a chapter in a grander narrative of love and restoration.

For I know that the One who formed me from the dust, who breathed life into my nostrils and placed me in the Garden of delight, has not abandoned His creation. The promise of a Savior, a second Adam who will undo the curse and restore the fellowship that was lost, burns like a beacon in the darkness of my regret.

And so, I cling to that promise, even as I bear the scars of my own disobedience. I whisper it to my children and my children's children, a legacy of hope amidst the thorns and thistles of a fallen world. And I trust that, in the fullness of time, the bitter fruit of knowledge will give way to the sweet wine of redemption, and all that was lost will be restored in the eternal Garden of grace.

# Chapter 24

# Jesus of Nazareth

## Reflections on an Unanswered Prayer

The night is heavy with the weight of sorrow, the garden of Gethsemane shrouded in a veil of darkness and despair. I, Jesus of Nazareth, the Son of God and the Savior of mankind, kneel alone in the shadows, my heart burdened with a regret that threatens to overwhelm my very soul.

For in this moment, as I face the crucible of my destiny, I am haunted by the memory of a prayer that went unanswered, a plea that seemed to fall on deaf ears in the halls of heaven. "My Father, if it is possible, let this cup pass from me," I had whispered into the stillness of the night, my spirit quailing at the thought of the suffering that lay ahead.

But even as the words left my lips, I knew that it was not to be. The cup of sorrow, the bitter draught of pain and death, was mine to drink to the dregs. And though I had always known that this was the path that I must walk, the way of the cross that would lead to the redemption of the world, I could not help but feel a sense of anguish at the thought of what lay ahead.

I think back to the years of my ministry, the countless lives that I had touched and transformed with my message of love and compassion. The lepers cleansed, the blind given sight, the dead raised to life again—these were the miracles that had marked my path, the signs and wonders that had borne witness to the power of God at work in the world.

But even as I had brought healing and hope to so many, I could not escape the knowledge that my own journey would be one of suffering and sorrow. The betrayal of Judas, the denial of Peter, the abandonment of my disciples in my hour of need—these were the wounds that cut deeper than any scourge or thorn, the pain that seared my soul even as my body was broken on the cross.

And yet, as I wrestle with the anguish of my own regret, I cannot help but wonder if there might have been another way. If the Father had answered my prayer, if the cup had passed from me, would the world still have been saved? Would the power of sin and death still have been broken, the gates of heaven thrown open to all who believed?

These are the questions that haunt me in the garden, the doubts that gnaw at the edges of my faith even as I submit to the will of the One who sent me. For though I know that my death is necessary, that my blood must be shed for the salvation of the world, I cannot help but feel the weight of all that might have been, the path not taken that might have led to a different end.

But even in the depths of my sorrow, I cling to the hope that my sacrifice will not be in vain. That the love that I have poured out for the world will be a balm for the wounds of humanity, a light in the darkness that will guide the lost and the broken back to the heart of God.

And so, I will drink the cup that is set before me, I will bear the cross that is mine to carry. I will endure the pain and the sorrow, the abandonment and the shame, knowing that through my suffering, the world will be redeemed, and the power of sin and death will be broken forever.

But as I go forth to meet my fate, I cannot help but offer one final prayer, one last plea to the Father who holds the world in his hands. Not a prayer for my own deliverance, but for the strength and the grace to endure what lies ahead, to bear the burden of my own regret with courage and with love.

"Father, forgive them," I whisper into the stillness of the night, my voice trembling with the weight of all that is to come. "For they know not what they do."

And though I know that the path ahead will be one of sorrow and pain, I trust in the love that has brought me this far, the love that will see me through to the end. For in the end, it is not my own will that matters, but the will of the One who sent me, the One who loves the world so much that he would give his only Son to die for its sake.

So let the story of my regret be a testament to the power of that love, a reminder that even in our darkest hours, we are never alone, never forsaken. And let the world know that through the pain and the sorrow, through the suffering and the sacrifice, there is always hope, always the promise of a new dawn, a new beginning in the light of God's unfailing grace.

# Chapter 25

# Judas Iscariot

# The Eternal Weight of Betrayal

In the darkest recesses of my soul, I am haunted by a decision that will torment me for all eternity. I, Judas Iscariot, the man whose name has become synonymous with betrayal, sit alone in the shadows, the weight of my treachery bearing down upon me like a millstone around my neck.

The silver pieces in my hand, once a symbol of opportunity and gain, now burn like hot coals, searing the flesh of my guilty palms. How could I have been so blind, so foolish, to think that any earthly reward could justify the betrayal of the one who called me friend, who chose me to walk beside him?

In the silence of my anguish, I am consumed by the memory of his eyes, the look of sorrow and resignation that pierced my very soul as I sealed his fate with a kiss. That moment, etched into the fabric of my being, will haunt me forever, a reminder of the terrible choice I made and the love I so carelessly discarded.

I had convinced myself that it was for the greater good, that Jesus' ministry had become a threat to the established order, a danger to the very foundations of our society. But in the cold light of truth, I see now that it was my own selfish ambition, my own desire for power and recognition, that drove me to make that fateful bargain.

And now, as I sit in the aftermath of my betrayal, I am overwhelmed by the magnitude of what I have done. I have condemned an innocent man, the Son of God himself, to a brutal and agonizing death. I have shattered the trust of those who called me brother, and I have turned my back on the one hope for redemption and salvation.

The weight of my sin is a burden too heavy to bear, a stain upon my soul that can never be washed clean. I am lost, cast adrift in a sea of my own making, with no hope of forgiveness or redemption.

In my despair, I sought to undo what could not be undone, to rid myself of the cursed silver and the guilt that clung to it like a disease. But even as I cast the money at the feet of those who had bought my betrayal, I knew that it was too late, that the die had been cast and the consequences of my actions could not be escaped.

And so, I wander now in the realm of eternal regret, a lost and tormented soul, forever separated from the light and love that I so foolishly spurned. The memory of my betrayal is a constant companion, a searing reminder of the choice that I made and the fate that I sealed.

But perhaps the greatest torment of all is the knowledge that my actions were not born of malice or hatred, but of weakness and fear. I loved Jesus, even as I betrayed him, and that realization is a dagger in my heart, a wound that will never heal.

And so, I am left to ponder the bitter irony of my fate, the knowledge that I, who was chosen to be a disciple of the Lord, will forever be remembered as the one who betrayed him. My name will be a curse upon the lips of the faithful, a cautionary tale of the dangers of greed and the consequences of turning one's back on the truth.

But even in the depths of my anguish, I cling to one final hope, one glimmer of light in the darkness. For I know that the story does not end with my betrayal, that the love I rejected and the truth I denied will ultimately triumph over sin and death.

And so, I watch from afar as the one I betrayed suffers and dies, as he takes upon himself the sins of the world and the weight of my own treachery. And in that moment, I finally understand the depth of the love that I had once scorned, the power of the grace that could have saved even one such as I.

But for me, it is too late. I am condemned to bear the weight of my regret for all eternity, to live with the knowledge that I had held the key to salvation in my hand and cast it aside for the sake of a few pieces of silver.

May my story stand as a warning to all who are tempted to betray their deepest convictions, to trade the eternal for the temporary. For the price of betrayal is a burden too heavy to bear, and the weight of regret will last forever.

# Chapter 26

# Dracula

# The Eternal Thirst for Meaning

In the silent depths of my castle, where the shadows dance to the rhythm of centuries past, I, Count Dracula, the immortal prince of darkness, find myself lost in the labyrinth of my own eternal regret. The blood that sustains my undead existence has long since turned to ashes in my mouth, a bitter reminder of the endless cycle of thirst and satiation that has defined my cursed being.

I think back to the early days of my transformation, when the promise of immortality and supernatural power first beckoned to me like a siren's call. I had been a man of ambition and passion, a warrior and a scholar who sought to leave his mark upon the world. But in my hubris, my desperate desire to transcend the limits of mortal existence, I succumbed to the dark arts, to the temptation of the forbidden and the profane.

And so, I emerged from the unholy rituals a changed being, my humanity stripped away and replaced by an insatiable hunger for blood and domination. At first, I reveled in my newfound powers, in the godlike ability to bend others to my will and to defy the very laws of nature. I stalked the night like a predator, taking what I desired without remorse or compassion, a true lord of the undead.

But as the centuries passed, and the weight of my immortality began to press down upon me like a suffocating shroud, I found myself consumed by a growing sense of emptiness and despair. The thrill of the hunt, the rush of power and control, began to pale in comparison to the gnawing absence of true meaning or purpose in my existence.

I watched as the world changed around me, as empires rose and fell, as the tides of history ebbed and flowed like the blood in my veins. And yet, I remained static, frozen in time, a relic of a bygone age condemned to an eternity of isolation and stagnation. The relationships I formed, the fleeting connections I made with the mortal world, were but pale imitations of the deep bonds of love and family that I had long since lost.

I began to question the very nature of my being, the dark gift that had once seemed like the key to unlocking the secrets of the universe. What was the point of immortality, of power and dominion, if it meant an endless existence devoid of growth, of change, of the very essence of what it meant to be alive? Had I, in my blind pursuit of the forbidden, traded the warmth of human connection for the cold embrace of the grave?

And then there were the innocents, the countless lives I had taken in my relentless pursuit of sustenance and power. In the beginning, I had justified my actions as the natural order of things, the strong preying upon the weak as they had done since the dawn of time. But as the weight of centuries pressed down upon me, and the faces of my victims began to haunt my waking dreams, I could no longer escape the bitter truth of my own monstrosity.

I had become the very thing I had once sought to transcend, a creature of darkness and despair, a blight upon the world that I had once hoped to conquer. And in my moments of deepest regret, I found myself longing for the release of true death, for the chance to finally lay down the burden of my cursed existence and find the peace that had eluded me for so long.

But even that final solace was denied to me, the price of my unholy bargain with the forces of darkness. And so, I continued to wander the earth, a specter of regret and longing, forever seeking the meaning and connection that had been lost to me in the moment of my transformation.

In the end, perhaps that is the true curse of the vampire, the eternal thirst for a life that can never be fully lived, the endless search for a soul that has long since been lost to the shadows. And though I may continue to stalk the night, to feed upon the blood of the living in a vain attempt to fill the void within, I know that I am forever doomed to the half-life of regret, the endless purgatory of a monster who has forgotten how to be human.

Let my story serve as a warning to those who would seek to cheat death, to those who would trade the precious gift of mortality for the false promise of eternal power. For in the end, the price of immortality is a thirst that can never be quenched, a hunger that can never be satisfied, and a regret that will haunt the soul for all eternity.

# Chapter 27

# Jack the Ripper

## The Haunting of Whitechapel

In the twilight of my days, as I wander the fog-shrouded streets of London, a specter of my own making, I am consumed by the weight of a guilt that knows no bounds. I, the faceless phantom whose deeds have haunted the pages of history, the monster of Whitechapel, the one they call Jack the Ripper.

The names of my victims, the women whose lives I so brutally cut short, echo in the chambers of my mind, a relentless litany of shame and sorrow. Mary Ann Nichols, Annie Chapman, Elizabeth Stride, Catherine Eddowes, Mary Jane Kelly—these are the ghosts that haunt my every waking moment, the indelible stains upon my blackened soul.

I think back to those nights of terror, the thrill of the hunt giving way to the frenzy of the kill, the momentary rush of power and control. In the heat of those moments, I felt a dark exultation, a sense of godlike dominion over life and death. But now, in the cold light of hindsight, I see the true depth of my depravity, the utter emptiness of my existence.

What twisted paths led me to become this thing, this dealer of death and destruction? What wounds, what traumas, what unspoken agonies lurked within me, fueling the fires of a madness that could not be contained? Even as I plumb the depths of my own history, searching for answers, I am faced with an impenetrable void.

The 'why' of my crimes may elude me, but the anguish they have left in their wake is an all-consuming reality. The shattered lives of family members and loved ones left behind, the festering sore of fear and unease that permeated London's East End, the simmering anger and grief that boiled over onto the streets.

And then there are the endless questions, the all-consuming mystery that has made my deeds a dark legend. The scrutiny of the public and the press, the rampant speculation and finger-pointing, the frustration of a police force stretched to the breaking point. In the eyes of the world, I am a cipher, a blank canvas onto which society projects its deepest fears and anxieties.

Perhaps it is fitting that I should remain unknown, a faceless embodiment of the darkness that lurks within the human heart. For in the end, my identity is less important than the lessons my crimes can teach us about the fragility of the social fabric, the price of poverty and marginalization, the consequences of unchecked rage and unhealed traumas.

And yet, even as I grapple with the enormity of my sins, I cannot help but wonder if redemption is possible, even for one such as I. Is there a path back from the abyss, a way to make amends for the lives I have shattered and the pain I have sown?

In the quiet moments of my solitude, I ponder these questions, silently begging for the mercy and forgiveness I know I do not deserve. The blood on my hands may never be washed clean, but perhaps, in some small way, my story can serve as a warning, a cautionary tale about the darkness that resides within us all, and the terrible price of succumbing to its siren song.

For in this life, we are all Whitechapel, all walking wounded in a world that can be cruel and unyielding. And it is only by confronting the shadows within ourselves, by facing the pain and the trauma with courage and compassion, that we can hope to find a measure of peace and healing.

So let my legacy be not one of fear and infamy, but of reckoning and revelation. Let my sins be laid bare so that others may learn from my mistakes, may choose a different path. And let the memory of my victims, the women whose lives I so selfishly stole, be forever honored, their voices lifted up as a clarion call for justice and change.

In this, perhaps, lies the key to my own redemption, the glimmer of light amidst the darkness. For only by shouldering the weight of my regrets, by using my story as a tool for transformation, can I hope to find some small measure of grace in the face of the unforgivable.

# Chapter 28

# Howard Carter

## The Curse of Tutankhamun's Tomb

In the dimly lit chambers of the Egyptian Museum, surrounded by the treasures of a long-dead king, I, Howard Carter, find myself haunted by the weight of a discovery that has come at a terrible cost. As I gaze upon the golden mask of Tutankhamun, the boy pharaoh whose tomb I uncovered, I am consumed by a sense of regret and sorrow, a feeling that the price of my own ambition may have been too high.

I think back to those early days of the expedition, when the Valley of the Kings seemed to hold endless possibilities, when the thrill of discovery was like a fire in my veins. I had devoted my life to the study of ancient Egypt, to unlocking the secrets of a civilization that had long since passed into legend. And when I finally stood before the sealed door of Tutankhamun's tomb, I felt a sense of destiny, a conviction that I was meant to be the one to bring this lost king back into the light.

But now, as I sit amidst the relics of that triumph, I am haunted by the realization that my own hubris may have unleashed a force beyond my control. The death of my dear friend and patron, Lord Carnarvon, just months after the opening of the tomb, was the first sign that something was amiss. He had been a constant companion and supporter, a man whose enthusiasm and generosity had made the expedition possible. And when he was struck down by a mysterious illness, I could not help but feel a sense of responsibility, a gnawing guilt that I had led him to his doom.

As the months passed and more members of the expedition began to fall ill or meet with strange accidents, the whispers of a curse began to grow louder. I tried to dismiss them as mere superstition, the ramblings of a sensationalist press and a public eager for a tale of mystery and intrigue. But in the dark hours of the night, when the museum was still and the shadows seemed to come alive, I could not escape the feeling that I had unleashed something dark and vengeful, a power that would stop at nothing to punish those who had dared to disturb the eternal slumber of the pharaohs.

I think of the ancient warnings that were inscribed upon the walls of the tomb, the dire pronouncements of the fate that would befall those who violated the sanctity of the king's resting place. I had dismissed them as mere superstition, the empty threats of a long-dead civilization. But now, as the body count mounts and the eerie coincidences pile up, I cannot help but wonder if there may have been some truth to those ancient curses, some malevolent force that I have unwittingly awakened.

And so, I am left to grapple with the bitter irony of my own success. I had sought to unlock the secrets of the past, to bring the glories of ancient Egypt to the world. But in doing so, I may have unleashed a darkness that threatens to consume us all, a curse that will haunt me and those I love for the rest of our days.

I think of the young pharaoh himself, the boy king whose eternal rest I have so rudely disturbed. I wonder what he would make of the chaos and controversy that has followed in the wake of his discovery, the media frenzy and the academic rivalries and the whispers of supernatural vengeance. Would he see it as a fitting tribute to his own greatness, a testament to the enduring power of his legacy? Or would he view it as a violation of the sacred trust that had been placed in me, a betrayal of the ancient laws and customs that had governed his world?

These are the questions that haunt me now, the doubts and regrets that gnaw at my soul even as I bask in the glow of my own achievement. I cannot escape the feeling that I have set in motion a chain of events that will echo through the ages, a curse that will forever be associated with my name and my legacy.

But perhaps that is the price of discovery, the burden that must be borne by those who seek to push the boundaries of human knowledge. Perhaps the curse of Tutankhamun is not some supernatural vengeance, but rather the weight of responsibility that comes with uncovering the secrets of the past, the realization that every great discovery comes with its own set of consequences and moral dilemmas.

And so, I must learn to live with the choices I have made, to bear the burden of my own success with grace and humility. I must honor the memory of those who have been lost, the friends and colleagues who have paid the ultimate price for my own ambition. And I must strive to use the knowledge and the treasures that I have uncovered for the greater good, to enlighten and inspire generations to come.

For that is the only way to truly honor the legacy of Tutankhamun and the civilization that he represents. Not by hiding from the consequences of our actions, but by embracing them, by using the lessons of the past to build a better future for all of humanity.

And though the regret and the sorrow may never fully fade, I know that I must press on, must continue to explore and discover and push the boundaries of what is possible. For that is the only way to truly do justice to the memory of those who have gone before, to honor the sacrifices that have been made in the name of knowledge and progress.

So let the curse of Tutankhamun be a reminder to us all, a warning of the price that must sometimes be paid for the pursuit of greatness. But let it also be a source of inspiration, a testament to the enduring power of the human spirit and the unquenchable thirst for understanding that drives us ever forward, even in the face of darkness and uncertainty.

# Chapter 29

# Robert Falcon Scott

## Reflections from the Frozen Edge of Oblivion

In the frigid embrace of the Antarctic, the wind howling a deafening dirge across the vast expanse of ice and snow, I, Captain Robert Falcon Scott, lie huddled in the tattered remains of a tent, my pencil clutched in frostbitten fingers as I etch the last entries of my expedition's fateful tale. The South Pole, that elusive prize which had beckoned me with its siren song of glory, now stands as a hollow triumph, forever eclipsed by the cruel shadow of my own failings.

As I stare into the frozen abyss that will soon become my tomb, I am consumed by the weight of my regrets, the decisions and choices that have led me and my loyal companions to this bitter end. The ghosts of my fallen comrades—Wilson, Bowers, Oates, and Evans—swirl around me, their silent reproach a searing indictment of my leadership and judgment.

I think back to the early days of our expedition, the Terra Nova steaming south from New Zealand, our hearts filled with hope and excitement at the prospect of making history. I had assembled a team of the finest men, each one a paragon of courage, skill, and determination. Together, we would conquer the continent's frozen heart and plant the British flag at the bottom of the world, a feat that would enshrine our names in the annals of glory, forever remembered for our valor and indomitable spirit.

But now, as I lie broken and shivering, the specter of death trailing its icy fingers down my spine, I am haunted by the realization that it was not the unforgiving elements that sealed our doom, but my own arrogance and stubbornness. In my relentless pursuit of the Pole, driven by the need to outshine that Norwegian Amundsen, I made a series of fateful decisions, rejecting the well-honed techniques of more experienced explorers in favor of my own flawed strategies.

The motorized sledges, those temperamental machines which had promised swift passage across the frozen wastes, instead became a hindrance, breaking down and sapping precious resources. The ponies, too, proved ill-suited to the extremity of the Antarctic cold, perishing in droves and leaving us to haul our own heavily-burdened sledges over crevasse-ridden terrain. If only I had heeded the lessons of my predecessors, the harsh wisdom earned through countless ordeals on this unforgiving continent. If only I had set aside my pride and embraced the ways of the Inuit, with their sled dogs and intimate knowledge of ice craft.

But it was not just in matters of transportation and technology that I erred so grievously. As a leader, I failed to adequately provide for the well-being of my men, underestimating the toll of the Antarctic's unrelenting savagery on both body and mind. The rations, so meticulously calculated in the warmth and comfort of London offices, proved woefully inadequate in the face of the grinding struggle of man hauling across hundreds of miles of ice. Scurvy, that ancient mariner's scourge, slowly sapped our strength, our bodies wasting away even as our resolve burned ever brighter.

And then there was Oates, brave, selfless Oates, whose final act of sacrifice will forever be seared into my memory. As gangrene ravaged his frostbitten feet, rendering each step an excruciating agony, he pleaded with us to leave him behind, to save ourselves and fulfill the glorious mission that had been entrusted to us. But in my unwavering commitment to never abandoning one of my own, I sealed his fate and those of us who remained.

"I am just going outside, and may be some time," he declared, before striding out into the raging blizzard, a lonely figure swallowed by the white void of oblivion. His noble sacrifice, born of love and loyalty to his fellow explorers, haunts me still, a testament to the indomitable human spirit in the face of unimaginable suffering.

As I write these final, faltering words, documenting my last breath for those who will one day discover our wind-scoured bodies in this icy tomb, I feel the weight of my failures bearing down upon me. It is my fervent hope that the record of our tragic tale will serve not just as a chronicle of our efforts, but as a warning and a lesson to future generations of explorers.

To those intrepid souls who will follow in our footsteps and venture into the frozen unknown, I offer this hard-earned wisdom: glory and ambition, when left unchecked, can be the most perilous of guides. It is resilience, humility, and an unwavering commitment to one's fellowship that forge the way through trials which defy human endurance.

I think of my wife, Kathleen, and our young son, Peter. The pain of knowing that I will never again feel the warmth of their embrace, never see the love that dances in their eyes as I regale them with tales of Antarctic wonders, is a bitter anguish sharper than the biting cold that devours my fading existence. It is for them, and for the hope that they represent, that my band of brothers and I embarked upon this fateful quest which will now stand as our epitaph.

As my strength ebbs and the gathering darkness closes in, I take small solace in having regained some measure of the humanity I had sacrificed in my monomaniacal pursuit of glory. That final great act of camaraderie and self-sacrifice by Edgar, Uncle Bill, and Birdie, huddled together against the unforgiving cold, refusing to leave one another's side even in the face of encroaching oblivion, serves as a balm to my battered soul.

May our tale endure not as a story of hubris and failure, but as a testament to the unbreakable bonds of fellowship forged in the crucible of shared hardship. May it remind those who come after us that it is not in conquest that we find our truest measure, but in the quiet moments of grace and compassion that flicker like fragile flames amidst the vast, uncaring expanse.

And though my earthly journey draws to a close here at the edge of the world, my spirit is unvanquished. For I have glimpsed the high sublime of human endeavor, and have learned, at the last, the true meaning of heroism—a steadfast devotion to one's comrades that endures even unto the frozen embrace of eternity.

May God bless and keep my Kathleen and dear Peter. May He watch over those brave souls who will someday follow the path we have broken. And may He grant me, in these final moments, the peace of knowing that though my life's ambition lies shattered amidst the unforgiving ice, I have found something far greater in the unwavering loyalty and love of those who lie beside me, bound until the end in glorious fellowship.

Thus do I, Robert Falcon Scott, with a steady hand but a heavy heart, consign these words as the last testament of my tragic yet transcendent Antarctic odyssey.

# Chapter 30

# Leopold Lojka

# The Burden of a Wrong Turn

In the quiet moments of the night, when the ghosts of the past come calling and the weight of history bears down upon my weary soul, I, Leopold Lojka, find myself transported back to that fateful day in Sarajevo—28 June 1914—the day when a single wrong turn changed the course of nations and sealed my fate as the unwitting instrument of catastrophe.

I was a young man then, a loyal servant of the Austro-Hungarian Empire, proud to be entrusted with the safety and security of the Archduke Franz Ferdinand and his beloved wife, Sophie. We had come to Sarajevo on a mission of peace and unity, a grand gesture to heal the divisions that threatened to tear our empire apart.

But from the moment we arrived in that troubled city, a sense of unease hung in the air, a palpable tension that set my nerves on edge. The streets were lined with sullen faces and hostile stares, and whispers of discontent and rebellion echoed in the shadows.

Then came the first attack, a grenade hurled at our motorcade by a Serbian nationalist, a harbinger of the chaos to come. By some miracle, the Archduke and his wife escaped unscathed, but several of our entourage were wounded, and the decision was made to visit them in the hospital.

It was then that fate dealt its cruel hand, and the course of history was forever altered. In the confusion of the moment, with adrenaline coursing through my veins and a thousand thoughts racing through my mind, I made a wrong turn, guiding the Archduke's car down a narrow side street, away from the safety of our planned route.

And there, as if lying in wait for us, was Gavrilo Princip, the assassin whose name would be forever etched into the annals of infamy. In that instant, as our eyes met and I saw the cold determination in his gaze, I knew that all was lost. The shots rang out, and the world stood still, as the Archduke and his wife slumped lifeless in the back seat, their blood staining my hands and my soul.

In the chaos and horror of that moment, as the weight of what had transpired began to sink in, I was gripped by a sense of overwhelming guilt and despair. How could I, who had been entrusted with the sacred duty of protection, have failed so utterly and completely? How could my simple mistake, a momentary lapse in judgment, have unleashed such a tide of death and destruction upon the world?

As the news of the assassination spread like wildfire, and the gears of war began to turn, I watched in helpless agony as the world I had known crumbled around me. Nations mobilized, alliances were invoked, and the flower of a generation marched off to die in the trenches and the fields of Europe.

And through it all, the burden of my guilt grew ever heavier, a millstone around my neck that dragged me down into the depths of despair. I saw the faces of the dead and the dying, the widows and the orphans, the shattered lives and broken dreams, and I knew that I bore a share of the blame for it all.

In the years that followed, as the war raged on and the toll of the carnage mounted, I sought desperately for some way to atone for my sin, to find redemption in a world gone mad. But everywhere I turned, I was haunted by the specter of that fateful day, the knowledge that my actions, however unintentional, had helped to unleash the dogs of war.

I thought of the Archduke and his wife, the two innocent souls whose lives had been so cruelly cut short, and I wept for the future they would never know, the children they would never raise, the love they would never share. And I thought of the millions of others, the countless lives shattered and destroyed by the conflict that my mistake had helped to ignite, and I felt the weight of their suffering pressing down upon my soul.

As the war ground on, and the hope of victory gave way to the grim reality of stalemate and attrition, I retreated into myself, a broken man haunted by the ghosts of the past. I sought solace in drink and solitude, trying to numb the pain of my guilt and the ache of my regrets.

But even in the darkest hours of my despair, I clung to the desperate hope that somehow, in some small way, my story might serve as a warning to those who would come after, a cautionary tale of the terrible consequences of a single moment's inattention, a reminder of the fragility of peace in a world forever poised on the brink of war.

And so, as I sit here in the twilight of my years, the last surviving witness to that fateful day in Sarajevo, I offer up my confession, a testament to the burden of guilt that I have borne for so long.

Let my story be remembered, not as a curiosity of history, but as a sobering reminder of the awesome responsibility that we all bear, the weight of our choices and the far-reaching consequences of our actions.

For in the end, the true lesson of my life is not the power of great men to shape the course of nations, but the terrible price that is paid when the small and the insignificant are forgotten, when the delicate balance of peace is shattered by the careless hand of fate.

And though I may never find the redemption that I seek, though the blood of the innocent may forever stain my hands, I can only pray that my story will serve as a beacon of hope in a world forever shadowed by the specter of war, a reminder that even in our darkest hours, the light of understanding and compassion can still guide us home.

# Chapter 31

# Gavrilo Princip

## The Bullet of No Regret

In the dank confines of my prison cell, as the inexorable grip of tuberculosis tightens around my lungs, I, Gavrilo Princip, find myself reflecting on the singular act that has defined my brief and tumultuous life. The shots that rang out on that fateful June day in Sarajevo, the bullets that felled the Archduke Franz Ferdinand and his wife, Sophie, echo still in the chambers of my memory, a testament to the unyielding force of my convictions.

As I sit here, awaiting the judgment of history and the merciful release of death, I am haunted not by regret for my actions, but by a fierce and unrelenting pride in the blow I struck against the oppressors of my people. For too long, we Serbs had languished under the yoke of Austro-Hungarian rule, our dreams of freedom and self-determination crushed beneath the boot of a foreign power.

I think back to the moment when I first resolved to take up the cause of Serbian liberation, to dedicate my life to the struggle for justice and independence. I was but a young student then, my head filled with the fiery ideals of nationalism and revolution, my heart burning with a righteous anger at the injustices inflicted upon my people.

And so, when the opportunity presented itself, when the heir to the Austro-Hungarian throne dared to set foot on the sacred soil of Sarajevo, I did not hesitate. With a steadiness of purpose that belied my years, I took aim and fired the shots that would change the course of history, that would set in motion a chain of events that would engulf the world in the flames of war.

Some may call me a terrorist, a fanatic, a madman. They may say that my actions were those of a misguided youth, a foolish idealist who did not understand the true consequences of his deeds. But I knew full well what I was doing, and I would do it again a thousand times over if it meant striking a blow for the cause of Serbian freedom.

And yet, even as I sit here, unwavering in my commitment to the righteousness of my cause, I cannot help but feel a twinge of sorrow for the suffering that my actions unleashed upon the world. I think of the millions of lives lost, the families torn asunder, the lands laid waste by the ravages of war. I think of my own people, the Serbs, who endured such hardship and persecution in the aftermath of my deed, their dreams of liberation dashed against the rocks of history.

In this, perhaps, lies the contrast between my own regrets and those of Leopold Lojka, the driver whose wrong turn sealed the fate of the Archduke and set the stage for my own fateful intervention. For Lojka, the regrets are those of a man caught up in the currents of history, a pawn in a game of power and politics beyond his understanding or control. His are the regrets of the unintended consequence, the tragic mistake that spirals out into a maelstrom of death and destruction.

But for me, the regrets are of a different order, born not of the unintended but of the all-too-intended, the deliberate and calculated act of resistance against an unjust order. I do not regret the choice I made, the path I took, for it was the only one that my conscience and my convictions would allow. But I do regret, perhaps, the price that others had to pay for my single-minded pursuit of justice, the devastation that my bullets unleashed upon a world that was not ready for the consequences of my actions.

And yet, even in the depths of this regret, I cannot help but feel a sense of hope, a glimmer of the dream that drove me to take up arms in the first place. For though the road to Serbian liberation has been long and fraught with hardship, though the sacrifices have been great and the victories hard-won, I know that my people will one day be free, that the seeds of revolution that I planted with my bullets will one day bear the fruit of self-determination.

And so, as I sit here in the gathering darkness, the last embers of my life flickering in the face of the inevitable, I offer these words not as an apology or a plea for forgiveness, but as a testament to the unyielding power of the human spirit, to the unquenchable thirst for freedom that burns in the hearts of all who suffer under the yoke of oppression.

Let my story be remembered, not as a cautionary tale of the dangers of youthful idealism, but as a clarion call to all who would take up the struggle for justice and liberty. Let my bullets be not a source of regret, but a spark of hope, a reminder that even in the darkest of times, there are those who are willing to lay down their lives for the dream of a better world.

And though my own part in this great drama may be drawing to a close, though my body may soon be consigned to the cold embrace of the grave, I know that my spirit will live on, a flame eternal in the hearts of all who continue the fight for freedom. For in the end, it is not the length of our lives that matters, but the depth of our commitment, the fire of our convictions, and the willingness to risk all for the sake of a cause greater than ourselves.

# Chapter 32

# T.E. Lawrence

# The Mirage of Arab Independence

In the echoes of the desert wind, amidst the shifting sands of a land I once called home, I, Thomas Edward Lawrence, find myself haunted by the bitter taste of a promise unfulfilled. The dream of an independent Arab nation, the cause for which I fought and sacrificed, remains a mirage on the horizon, forever out of reach.

forever out of reach.

I think back to those years of fire and blood, when the world was consumed by the Great War, and the fate of empires hung in the balance. As a young British officer, I found myself drawn into the heart of the Arab Revolt, a witness to and participant in a struggle for freedom and self-determination.

From the vast expanses of the Hejaz to the ancient streets of Damascus, I rode alongside the sons of the desert, men who had taken up arms against the Ottoman oppressors. In their eyes, I saw the flicker of a dream, the longing for a land they could call their own, free from the yoke of foreign domination.

And I, in my naivete and idealism, believed that I could help make that dream a reality. I leveraged my position, my knowledge, my influence, to rally support for the Arab cause, to convince the powers that be that the time had come for a new order in the Middle East.

But even as I negotiated and maneuvered, as I poured my heart and soul into the campaign for Arab independence, the seeds of betrayal were being sown behind closed doors. The Sykes-Picot Agreement, that cynical carving up of the region by European powers, laid bare the true nature of the game being played.

I watched in horror as the promises made to the Arabs were cast aside, as the dream of a unified and independent Arab state was shattered into a thousand pieces. The land I had come to love, the people I had fought beside, were to be divided and ruled, their fate decided by men in faraway capitals who cared little for their aspirations.

The weight of that betrayal, the knowledge that I had been a pawn in a game far larger than myself, haunts me to this day. I think of the lives lost, the sacrifices made, the hopes and dreams that were crushed beneath the wheels of realpolitik. And I cannot help but feel a deep and abiding sense of regret, a gnawing guilt that I did not do more, that I could not keep the promises I had made.

In the end, I was forced to confront the bitter truth that the world of empires and alliances, of Great Powers and spheres of influence, had little room for the aspirations of those who dared to dream of something different. The Arab Revolt, for all its romance and heroism, was but a footnote in the larger story of the war and its aftermath.

And yet, even as I grapple with the weight of my own failures and the broken promises of history, I cannot bring myself to regret the journey I undertook, the bonds I forged, the cause I championed. For in the struggle for Arab independence, I found a sense of purpose, a calling that transcended the narrow confines of my own life.

I may have failed to bring about the dream of a united Arab nation, but I like to believe that the spirit of that dream, the yearning for freedom and self-determination, lives on in the hearts of those who continue to fight for a better future. And perhaps, in some small way, my own story, my own witness to the bravery and resilience of the Arab people, will serve as an inspiration to those who come after.

For in the end, the true measure of a life is not in the victories won or the defeats suffered, but in the courage to stand up for what one believes, to risk all in the name of a higher ideal. And though the dream of Arab independence remains unfulfilled, I know that the struggle for justice and freedom is one that will endure, as long as there are those willing to take up the mantle and carry the fight forward.

So let the sands of Arabia bear witness to my regret, to the promise that was broken and the hope that was lost. But let them also testify to the unbreakable spirit of a people who refuse to be denied their birthright, who will continue to strive for the dignity and self-determination that is the inalienable right of all humanity.

And let my own story, the tale of a man caught between worlds, serve as a reminder of the complex web of loyalties and betrayals that so often shape the course of history. For it is only by confronting the hard truths of the past that we can hope to build a future worthy of the sacrifices made and the dreams deferred.

In the haunting echoes of the Arabian wind, I hear the whisper of a promise that remains unfulfilled, a dream that still beckons from beyond the distant horizon. And though I may not live to see its realization, I know that the struggle for Arab independence, for the right of a people to chart their own destiny, is one that will endure, as long as there are those who hold fast to the belief that a better world is possible.

# Chapter 33
# Tsar Nicholas II
## The Last Romanov's Lament

In the suffocating darkness of my captivity, I, Tsar Nicholas II, the last Emperor and Autocrat of All the Russias, find myself haunted by the specter of my own failings. As the walls of this house-turned-prison close in around me, I am left to ponder the decisions that brought me to this moment, the choices that sealed the fate of my dynasty and my beloved country.

I was born into a world of unimaginable privilege and power, the anointed sovereign of a vast empire stretching across two continents. From my earliest days, I was raised to believe in the divine right of kings, the unquestionable authority of the monarchy, and the sacred duty to uphold the traditions of my forefathers.

But as I sit here, stripped of my titles and my freedom, I am forced to confront the painful truth that it was my own stubborn adherence to those very traditions that brought about my downfall. I failed to see the gathering storm on the horizon, the rising tide of discontent among my people, the yearning for change and progress in a world that was rapidly leaving the old order behind.

I think back to the early days of my reign, when the challenges facing our nation seemed surmountable. I had grand visions of a Russia that was both mighty and just, a land where the nobility and the peasantry could live in harmony under the benevolent guidance of the tsar. But as the years passed and the pressures mounted, I found myself increasingly out of touch with the realities of my own country.

I surrounded myself with sycophants and flatterers, advisors who told me only what I wanted to hear. I ignored the warnings of those who saw the growing unrest, the whispers of revolution that were spreading like wildfire among the workers and the intelligentsia. I believed that the love of my people was unshakable, that the bonds between the tsar and his subjects were eternal and unbreakable.

How wrong I was. When the revolution came, it was like a force of nature, sweeping away centuries of tradition and privilege in a matter of days. I watched helplessly as my army crumbled, as my most trusted advisors fled or turned against me, as the very foundations of my world came crashing down around me.

In the end, I was left with nothing but the bitter realization of my own failures. I had been a prisoner of my own narrow-mindedness, a slave to the dogmas and prejudices of a bygone era. I had failed to lead my country into the modern age, to adapt to the changing times and the evolving needs of my people.

And now, as I face an uncertain fate in this bleak and lonely place, I am haunted by the weight of my own mistakes. I think of the countless lives that were lost in the chaos of the revolution, the families torn apart by violence and upheaval, the dreams and aspirations that were shattered on the altar of history.

I think of my own family, my beloved wife and children, who have been forced to share in my disgrace and my suffering. I think of the legacy that I leave behind, the tarnished crown of the Romanovs, the once-great dynasty reduced to ashes and memory.

But perhaps most of all, I am haunted by the realization that I could have been a different kind of ruler, a tsar who listened to his people and worked to build a better future for all. I had the power and the resources to make a difference, to lead Russia into a new era of prosperity and progress. But I was too afraid, too stubborn, too beholden to the traditions of the past to seize that opportunity.

And so, I am left with nothing but regret, the bitter fruit of a life lived in the shadow of my own failures. I can only hope that future generations will learn from my mistakes, that they will find the wisdom and the courage to build a Russia that is truly free and just, a nation that honors the dreams and aspirations of all its people.

For that is the only legacy that matters, the only way to redeem the sins of the past and build a better world for those who come after us. And though my own story may be one of tragedy and failure, I pray that it will also be a cautionary tale, a reminder of the perils of unchecked power and the importance of listening to the voices of the people.

As I sit here in the gathering darkness, I can only offer a silent prayer for the future of my beloved Russia, and for the souls of all those who have suffered and sacrificed in the name of a dream that I was too blind to see. May they find the peace and the justice that I could not give them, and may their memory be a guiding light for generations to come.

# Chapter 34

# Alexander Kerensky

# The Shattered Vision of a Democratic Russia

In the solitude of exile, I, Alexander Kerensky, find myself haunted by the ghosts of a revolution that slipped through my fingers. As the once-great hope of Russian democracy, I bear the weight of a dream that turned to ashes in my hands, a vision of a free and just society that was consumed by the fires of radicalism and despotism.

I think back to those heady days of 1917, when the world seemed to be on the brink of a new era, a time of unprecedented change and possibility. As the leader of the Provisional Government, I felt the weight of history on my shoulders, the responsibility to guide my country through the treacherous waters of political and social upheaval.

But even as I worked tirelessly to build a new Russia, to create a government that was accountable to the people and responsive to their needs, I found myself beset on all sides by the forces of extremism and intolerance. The Bolsheviks, with their seductive promises of a workers' paradise, were gathering strength by the day, while the reactionary elements of the old order plotted to restore the monarchy and crush the nascent democracy.

I believed with all my heart in the power of moderation and compromise, in the need to find a middle path between the competing visions of left and right. I thought that by bringing all the factions together, by forging a consensus around the basic principles of democratic governance, we could create a Russia that was both free and stable, a beacon of hope for the oppressed masses of Europe and beyond.

But I underestimated the depth of the divisions that ran through our society, the bitterness and resentment that had been simmering for generations. I failed to see the warning signs, the growing radicalization of the workers and soldiers, the erosion of support for the Provisional Government among the intelligentsia and the middle classes.

And when the moment of truth came, when the Bolsheviks seized power in the October Revolution, I found myself powerless to stop them. My appeals for calm and restraint fell on deaf ears, my calls for a united front against the forces of tyranny were drowned out by the clamor of extremism and violence.

In the end, I was forced to flee, to watch from afar as the country I loved descended into the abyss of civil war and dictatorship. And now, as I sit in the twilight of my life, I am haunted by the knowledge that I could have done more, that I should have been stronger and more decisive in the face of the challenges that confronted us.

I think of the countless lives that were lost in the years of bloodshed and repression that followed, the dreams and aspirations that were crushed under the boot of totalitarianism. I think of the legacy of the Soviet Union, the long shadow of fear and oppression that hung over Russia for generations, the scars that still linger on the soul of our nation.

And I am consumed by the bitter realization that I bear a share of the responsibility for that tragedy. I was the one who had the chance to lead Russia to a better future, to build a society based on the principles of freedom, democracy, and human rights. But I let that chance slip away, I allowed myself to be outmaneuvered and outfought by those who sought to impose their own vision of utopia by force.

This is my burden, the regret that I will carry with me to my grave. The knowledge that I could have been the one to save Russia from the horrors of the 20th century, that I could have been the champion of a democratic revolution that would have changed the course of history.

But I failed, and the price of that failure was paid in the blood and tears of millions. I can only hope that future generations will learn from my mistakes, that they will find the courage and the wisdom to build a Russia that is truly free and just, a nation that honors the dreams and aspirations of all its people.

For that is the only way to redeem the sins of the past, to honor the memory of those who suffered and died in the name of a better world. And though my own story may be one of tragedy and regret, I pray that it will also be a source of inspiration, a reminder of the enduring power of the democratic ideal and the unquenchable thirst for freedom that lies in the heart of every human being.

As I sit here in the gathering twilight, I can only offer a silent prayer for the future of Russia, and for the souls of all those who have struggled and sacrificed in the name of that ideal. May they find the peace and the justice that I could not give them, and may their memory be a guiding light for generations to come.

# Chapter 35

# Vladimir Lenin

## The Weight of the Red Star

In the twilight of my life, as I lie confined to this bed, my once-indomitable body ravaged by the bullets of a would-be assassin, I, Vladimir Ilyich Ulyanov, known to the world as Lenin, find myself haunted by the weight of my own creation. The revolution that I fought so hard to bring about, the dream of a world freed from the shackles of oppression and inequality, has taken on a life of its own, and I fear that it may not be the utopia I once envisioned.

I think back to those early days, when the fire of Marxism first ignited in my heart, when I believed with every fiber of my being that the workers of the world would rise up and throw off the chains of their capitalist overlords. I dedicated my life to this cause, enduring exile and hardship, always keeping my eyes fixed on the ultimate prize: a society where the proletariat would rule, where the fruits of labor would be shared equally among all.

And then, miraculously, it happened. The revolution came, and the old order crumbled. The Tsar was overthrown, and the Provisional Government was swept aside. I returned to Russia, hailed as a hero by the masses, the leader who would guide them into a bright new future.

But as I took the reins of power, as I sought to mold the nascent Soviet state into the image of my dreams, I began to realize the true magnitude of the task before me. The challenges were immense, the obstacles seemingly insurmountable. The country was in ruins, ravaged by war and famine, the people exhausted and disillusioned.

I believed that the key to building socialism lay in the strict control of the state over all aspects of life, in the suppression of dissent and the elimination of any potential threats to the revolution. I established the Cheka, the secret police that would become a symbol of terror and repression. I ordered the execution of the Tsar and his family, a ruthless act that I justified as a necessary step to secure the future of the revolution.

But as the years passed and the Soviet Union took shape, as I watched the bureaucracy grow and the Party tighten its grip on power, I began to feel a creeping sense of unease. The socialism we were building was not the one I had envisioned, not the one that would free the workers and create a truly egalitarian society.

Instead, I saw a new elite emerging, a class of Party officials and apparatchiks who wielded power with the same ruthless efficiency as the capitalists of old. I saw the suppression of free thought and artistic expression, the stifling of any voice that dared to question the Party line. I saw the gulags filling up with those deemed enemies of the state, the forced collectivization of agriculture that led to the deaths of millions.

And now, as I lie here in the shadow of death, I am haunted by the realization that perhaps I made a terrible mistake. Perhaps in my zeal to create a perfect society, I unleashed forces that I could not control, forces that would lead to the betrayal of the very ideals I held so dear.

I think of the power struggles that are already brewing among my successors, the jockeying for position and influence that threatens to tear apart the very fabric of the Party. I think of Stalin, the man who I once saw as my most loyal disciple, but who I now fear may become the embodiment of everything I fought against—a brutal dictator who will stop at nothing to maintain his grip on power.

And I am filled with a sense of profound regret, a realization that perhaps the revolution I fought for was doomed from the start, that the seeds of its own destruction were planted in the very methods we used to bring it about. The violence, the repression, the intolerance of dissent—these were the tools we wielded in the name of liberation, but they have only served to create a new tyranny in place of the old.

As I feel my life slipping away, I am haunted by the thought that I may have led my beloved Russia down a path from which there is no return. That the socialist paradise I dreamed of may never come to pass, that the sacrifices of so many may have been in vain.

But even in my darkest moments of doubt, I cling to the hope that perhaps, in some distant future, the true spirit of the revolution will be rekindled. That a new generation will take up the banner of socialism and carry it forward, learning from our mistakes and building a society that truly embodies the ideals of equality and justice.

For though I may have failed in my own lifetime, though the revolution I fought for may have been betrayed, I still believe in the power of the human spirit to overcome even the greatest of obstacles. I still believe that a better world is possible, that the workers of the world will one day unite and break the chains of their oppressors.

And so, I go to my grave with a heavy heart, burdened by the weight of my own regrets, but also with a flicker of hope for the future. A hope that my life and my struggle will not have been in vain, that the lessons of the past will be learned and that the dream of a truly just and equal society will one day become a reality.

Let history be my judge, and let the generations to come learn from my triumphs and my failures alike. For in the great march of human progress, every step counts, and even the most flawed and fallible among us have a role to play in the shaping of a better tomorrow.

# Chapter 36
# Mikhail Gorbachev
## The Last Soviet Dreamer

As I sit in the quietude of my Moscow home, the once-vibrant halls of the Kremlin now consigned to the annals of history, I, Mikhail Sergeyevich Gorbachev, find myself reflecting on the tumultuous years that reshaped the world and redefined my legacy. The mantle of leadership, once a beacon of hope and a promise of change, now feels like a heavy burden, a reminder of the dreams unfulfilled and the costs of a revolution unfinished.

I remember the early days of my tenure as General Secretary, a time of great anticipation and fervor. The Soviet Union, the mighty superpower that had held the world in its thrall for decades, was at a crossroads, its stagnant economy and ossified political system in desperate need of reform. I saw in this moment an opportunity to chart a new course, to unleash the creative energies of our people and to build a socialism with a human face.

Thus began the great experiment of perestroika and glasnost, the twin pillars of my vision for a renewed and revitalized Soviet Union. I sought to open up our society, to allow for greater freedom of expression and to encourage a new spirit of innovation and entrepreneurship. I believed that by loosening the reins of state control and allowing for a measure of dissent and debate, we could breathe new life into the socialist project and secure its future for generations to come.

But as the winds of change began to gather strength, I found myself buffeted by forces beyond my control. The long-suppressed nationalist sentiments of the Soviet republics, once held in check by the iron fist of the Communist Party, now burst forth with a vengeance, threatening to tear apart the very fabric of our union. The hardliners within the party, alarmed by the pace and scope of the reforms, began to push back, seeking to preserve their privileges and to sabotage the process of change.

I think back to those fateful days of August 1991, when the reactionary forces within the government launched their ill-fated coup attempt. As I sat imprisoned in my Crimean dacha, cut off from the levers of power and the support of my allies, I could only watch in horror as the fragile gains of the previous years began to unravel. Though the coup was ultimately defeated, the damage had been done, and the centrifugal forces of nationalism and separatism had been unleashed, setting the stage for the final dissolution of the Soviet Union.

In the years since, as I have watched the once-mighty superpower splinter into a patchwork of independent states, each grappling with its own challenges and contradictions, I have been forced to confront the painful question of my own role in this historic upheaval. Did I move too quickly, pushing for change at a pace that our society was not ready to absorb? Did I underestimate the depth of the economic and social crisis that had taken root in the waning years of Soviet power?

These are the doubts that haunt me in the quiet moments of introspection, the regrets that gnaw at the edges of my conscience. I think of the millions of our citizens who were plunged into poverty and despair in the chaotic years of the post-Soviet transition, the once-proud workers and intellectuals reduced to penury and desperation. I think of the lost opportunities for cooperation and partnership with the West, the squandered chances to build a new and more equitable world order in the aftermath of the Cold War.

And yet, even as I grapple with the weight of my own decisions and the consequences of my actions, I cannot help but feel a sense of pride in what we sought to achieve, in the bold vision of a society transformed by the power of ideas and the courage of conviction. For in the end, the true measure of a leader lies not in the accolades of the moment, but in the seeds of change that are planted for the future, the sparks of hope that are kindled in the hearts of a generation.

Though the Soviet Union may be no more, and though the path to a more just and humane socialism may be strewn with obstacles and setbacks, I remain convinced that the ideals that animated our struggle, the dreams of a world freed from the shackles of oppression and exploitation, will never die. For as long as there are those who believe in the power of human solidarity and the imperative of social justice, the legacy of our imperfect but historic experiment will endure.

And so, as I reflect on the arc of my own life and the fate of the nation I once led, I offer these words not as a final verdict, but as an invitation to continue the work that we began, to take up the banner of change and to carry it forward into an uncertain but hopeful future. For though the road may be long and the challenges daunting, I am convinced that a better world is possible, and that the seeds of that world lie in the struggles and sacrifices of all those who dare to dream of a different tomorrow.

# Chapter 37
# King Edward VIII
# The King Who Chose Love

In the quiet moments of my exile, as I look out upon the rolling hills of the French countryside, I, Edward VIII, the man who once sat upon the throne of England, find myself haunted by the echoes of a decision that changed the course of history. Though I have never regretted choosing love over the crown, I cannot escape the weight of the consequences that followed, the ripples of my actions that spread far beyond the confines of my own heart.

I think back to that fateful day, when I stood before the nation and declared my intention to abdicate, to forsake the duty and destiny that had been mine since birth. In that moment, I felt a sense of liberation, a glorious freedom in choosing my own path, in following the dictates of my soul rather than the expectations of the world.

But even as I reveled in the joy of my newfound love, the woman for whom I had given up everything, I could not ignore the storm that was brewing, the turmoil that my choice had unleashed upon the monarchy and the nation I had sworn to serve.

I watched as my beloved brother, George, was thrust into a role he had never sought, burdened with the weight of a crown that should have been mine. I saw the strain on his face, the weariness in his eyes, as he took on the mantle of kingship in a time of great uncertainty and upheaval.

And though I knew that he would rise to the challenge, that he would serve with the same dedication and devotion that had always been his hallmark, I could not help but feel a twinge of guilt, a sense that I had placed an unfair burden upon his shoulders.

I think of the disappointment in my mother's eyes, the stony silence of my father, as I told them of my intention to marry Wallis Simpson. The realization that I had shattered their dreams for me, that I had chosen a path that they could neither understand nor approve, was a bitter pill to swallow.

And yet, even in the face of their disapproval, their anger and their sorrow, I could not bring myself to regret my choice. For in Wallis, I had found a love that transcended all earthly considerations, a bond that could not be broken by the chains of duty or the weight of tradition.

But as the years passed and the world moved on, I began to see the deeper implications of my abdication, the constitutional crisis that I had unwittingly set in motion. The realization that my personal choice had shaken the very foundations of the monarchy, that it had called into question the role and relevance of the crown in a changing world, was a sobering one.

I watched from afar as my country faced the darkest hours of its history, as the specter of war loomed on the horizon and the nation turned to its king for guidance and strength. And though I knew that George would rise to the occasion, that he would be the leader that England needed in its hour of need, I could not escape the nagging sense that I had abandoned my duty, that I had left my people in their time of greatest peril.

These are the regrets that haunt me now, the burdens that I will carry with me to the end of my days. Not for the love that I chose or the life that I built with Wallis, but for the unintended consequences of my actions, the pain and the turmoil that I wrought upon those I held most dear.

And yet, even in the depths of my regret, I cannot bring myself to wish that I had chosen differently. For the love that Wallis and I shared was a once-in-a-lifetime gift, a flame that burned too brightly to be extinguished by the winds of duty or the tides of history.

In the end, I can only hope that my story will serve as a reminder of the true nature of love, of the sacrifices that we make and the prices that we pay in the pursuit of our heart's desire. And though my abdication may have shaken the foundations of the monarchy, though it may have caused pain and upheaval for those I left behind, I know that it was a choice born of authenticity, of the unshakable conviction that love must always triumph over duty.

So let my legacy be one of a man who dared to follow his heart, who chose the thorny crown of love over the gilded cage of tradition. And let the ripples of my choice, the consequences that I could not foresee, stand as a testament to the enduring power of the human spirit, to the courage and the conviction that drives us all to seek our own destiny, no matter the cost.

# Chapter 38

# Vladimir Horowitz

## The Dissonance of Perfection

The ivory keys beckon to me, their cool smoothness a siren's call to my tortured soul. I, Vladimir Horowitz, once hailed as the greatest pianist of my generation, now sit in the shadows of my own despair, haunted by the ghosts of a life lived in the relentless pursuit of perfection.

As my fingers hover over the keyboard, I am transported back to the early days of my career, when the world lay at my feet and the music flowed from me like a river of pure emotion. I had the power to move audiences to tears, to transport them to realms of ecstasy and wonder, to make them believe in the transformative power of art.

But even then, in the midst of my greatest triumphs, I could feel the seeds of my own destruction taking root. The pressure to be perfect, to live up to the impossible standards I set for myself, began to eat away at my very core, like a cancer of the soul.

I think of the countless hours I spent practicing, honing my craft to a razor's edge, sacrificing everything in the name of my art. My relationships, my health, my very sanity—all were laid upon the altar of the piano, a sacrifice to the gods of music and ambition.

And yet, no matter how hard I worked, no matter how flawless my technique or how profound my interpretations, I could never escape the gnawing feeling that it was never enough. There was always one more note to perfect, one more nuance to capture, one more peak to scale in the unending quest for artistic sublimity.

As the years passed and my fame grew, so too did my inner turmoil. The stage fright that had always plagued me became an all-consuming terror, a beast that lurked in the wings, waiting to devour me whole. I began to withdraw from the world, to retreat into a fortress of solitude and despair, convinced that I was unworthy of the accolades and adulation that had once sustained me.

And then came the breakdowns, the bouts of depression and anxiety that left me shattered and broken, a mere shell of the man I had once been. I watched as my career crumbled around me, as the music that had once been my lifeblood became a source of unending torment and pain.

In my darkest moments, I couldn't help but wonder if it had all been worth it. The sacrifices, the suffering, the unending pursuit of an ideal that always seemed to slip through my fingers like grains of sand. Had I traded my very humanity for a fleeting moment of glory, a brief taste of immortality that left me forever grasping for more?

And yet, even in the depths of my despair, I could not let go of the music. It was the one constant in my life, the one thing that gave meaning to my existence, even as it threatened to destroy me from within. I clung to it like a drowning man to a life raft, convinced that if I could just find my way back to that place of pure artistry, all would be well once more.

But now, as I sit in the twilight of my years, I am haunted by the realization that the price of perfection may have been too high. The relationships I neglected, the joys I missed out on, the simple pleasures of a life lived in the moment—all were sacrificed on the altar of my own ambition, my own insatiable need to be the best.

And so, I am left with nothing but regret, a bitter taste in my mouth that no amount of applause or adulation can ever erase. The dissonance of my own existence, the clash between the beauty I sought to create and the ugliness of the means by which I pursued it, will haunt me to my dying day.

But perhaps that is the true nature of art—a mirror that reflects back to us the very best and worst of ourselves, a crucible in which we are tested and transformed, even as we seek to transform the world around us. And though the price may be high and the path fraught with peril, I cannot help but believe that it is a journey worth taking, a struggle that ennobles even as it destroys.

For ultimately, the music is all that matters. And though I may have lost myself along the way, I know that somewhere, in the soaring melodies and shimmering harmonies of the great composers, I will always find my way back home.

# Chapter 39

# Henry Tandey

# Haunted by the Ghost of Hitler

The mud of the battlefield clings to my boots as I trudge through the trenches, the weight of my rifle a familiar burden. The screams of the dying and the thunder of artillery have become the soundtrack of my existence, a relentless reminder of the horror that surrounds me.

But it is not the carnage of war that haunts me now, as I sit in the quiet of my home, medals gleaming on my chest. It is a single moment, a decision made in the heat of battle, that weighs upon my soul like a millstone.

I close my eyes and I am back in that ditch, the acrid smell of gunpowder filling my nostrils. 1914. The soldier before me, his uniform tattered and stained with blood, his eyes wide with fear. In that instant, I saw not an enemy, but a fellow human being, a man no different from myself.

My finger hovered over the trigger, the power to end a life resting in the crook of my finger. But something stayed my hand, a flicker of compassion, a recognition of the humanity that exists even in the darkest of moments.

I lowered my rifle, watching as the man limped away, his fate now entwined with my own. Little did I know then the path that he would choose, the darkness that would consume him.

Adolf Hitler. The name that would come to embody the very evil I fought against, the monster who plunged the world into the abyss of another war. And I, Henry Tandey, had held his life in my hands.

The knowledge of what might have been gnaws at me, a festering wound that will not heal. Could I have changed the course of history with a single bullet? Could I have prevented the suffering of millions, the atrocities that stain the pages of our history books?

I am haunted by the faces of those who perished in the Holocaust, the innocent lives snuffed out by the madness of one man. And I cannot help but feel the weight of responsibility, the burden of mercy that I granted in that fateful moment.

Yet, even as I grapple with the enormity of my decision, I cannot bring myself to regret the compassion that stayed my hand. For in that moment, I acted not as a soldier, but as a human being. I chose to see the humanity in my enemy, to offer a glimmer of hope in a world consumed by darkness.

Perhaps it is not my place to play God, to determine who lives and who dies. Perhaps the burden of history is too great for any one man to bear.

But I will carry this weight, this regret, as a reminder of the power of a single act of mercy. For in the end, it is our humanity that defines us, that lights the way in the darkest of times.

And so I will continue to bear witness, to tell my story, in the hope that others may learn from my choices. That they may understand the true cost of war, the price of compassion in a world torn asunder.

For in the end, we are all soldiers in the battle for our souls, each of us bearing the scars of the choices we make. And it is only by embracing our humanity, by recognizing the divine spark that resides within us all, that we can hope to find peace in a world at war.

# Chapter 40

# Oskar Schindler

## The Redemption of a Righteous Man

In the quiet moments of introspection, when the weight of memory bears down upon my soul, I, Oskar Schindler, find myself grappling with the choices that have come to define my life. The hero, the savior, the man who risked everything to snatch more than a thousand Jewish lives from the jaws of the Nazi death machine—this is the legacy that will forever be attached to my name. But beneath the veneer of righteousness, there lies a darker truth, a past that I cannot escape, a burden of guilt and regret that I will carry with me to my final days.

I think back to the early years of the war, when the promise of power and profit drew me into the ranks of the Nazi Party. As a young industrialist, eager to make my mark in the world, I saw in Hitler's regime an opportunity to advance my own interests, to build a business empire on the backs of the conquered and the oppressed. I closed my eyes to the suffering and the injustice, convinced myself that I was merely a cog in the machine, a passive observer of the great tide of history.

But as the true horrors of the Nazi agenda began to unfold, as I witnessed firsthand the brutal treatment of the Jews in my own factory, I found myself confronted with a moral awakening, a gradual realization of the depths of my own complicity. The haunted eyes of the prisoners, the emaciated bodies and the scarred souls—these were the human costs of my own ambition, the price of my willful blindness.

And so began my journey of redemption, my desperate quest to save as many lives as I could from the gas chambers and the crematoria. I poured my fortune into bribes and black market deals, used my influence and my cunning to keep my Jewish workers safe from the clutches of the SS. I watched as the names on my list grew longer and longer, a fragile lifeline in a sea of death and despair.

But even as I worked tirelessly to protect the lives of those in my care, I could not shake the gnawing sense of guilt, the knowledge that for every soul I saved, countless others were lost to the abyss. I thought of the ones I could not reach, the families torn apart, the children ripped from their mothers' arms, the ash and smoke that choked the skies over Auschwitz and Treblinka.

And I thought too of my own role in the machinery of death, the ways in which my own actions, however well-intentioned, were still inextricably linked to the larger horrors of the Holocaust. For even as I fought to save lives, I was still a part of the system that had set out to destroy them, still a beneficiary of the cruel calculus of genocide.

In the years that followed, as the world struggled to come to terms with the incomprehensible scale of the Nazi atrocities, I found myself haunted by the weight of my own past, the specter of the choices I had made and the lives I had failed to save. The accolades and the honors, the gratitude of those I had rescued—none of it could erase the stain of my own complicity, the bitter knowledge that I could have done more, should have done more.

And yet, even in the depths of my regret, I cling to the hope that my story, however imperfect and incomplete, might serve as a beacon of light in a world still shadowed by the horrors of the past. For if a man like me, a once-ardent Nazi and a profiteer of war, could be transformed by the power of compassion and the call of conscience, then perhaps there is still hope for humanity, still a chance for redemption in the face of even the darkest of evils.

Let my journey stand as a testament to the enduring resilience of the human spirit, to the capacity for change and growth that lies within each of us. And let it also serve as a warning, a reminder of the terrible price of silence and indifference in the face of injustice, a call to action for all those who would stand against the forces of hatred and oppression.

It is not the grand gestures or the heroic deeds that define our lives, but the small, daily choices we make, the quiet acts of courage and compassion that light the way forward in a world too often consumed by darkness. And though I may have failed to live up to that ideal in my own past, I take solace in the knowledge that my legacy, however flawed and imperfect, has helped to keep alive the flame of hope and humanity in the face of unimaginable evil.

So let us remember the lessons of the Holocaust, the terrible toll of hatred and indifference, and let us also remember the power of individual action, the capacity for even the most unlikely of heroes to make a difference in the world. For it is only by confronting the darkness within ourselves, by embracing the call to compassion and justice, that we can hope to build a future worthy of those who were lost, a world in which the righteous deeds of the few can triumph over the sins of the many.

# Chapter 41

# Neville Chamberlain

# The Man Who Sought Peace

As I sit in the quiet of my study, the weight of the world bearing down upon my weary shoulders, I, Neville Chamberlain, find myself haunted by the specter of a peace that slipped through my grasp. The years have passed, the tides of war have ebbed and flowed, and yet the bitter taste of regret lingers still upon my tongue, a testament to the folly of a man who dared to dream of a world without conflict.

I think back to those fateful days in Munich, when the eyes of the world were fixed upon me, the champion of appeasement, the architect of a new era of understanding between nations. I remember the surge of hope that swelled within my breast as I stood beside Herr Hitler, the embodiment of a resurgent Germany, and put pen to paper, sealing a pact that I believed would usher in a golden age of tranquility.

"Peace for our time," I declared, holding aloft that precious scrap of paper, the Munich Agreement, as if it were a holy relic, a talisman against the gathering storms of war. In that moment, I truly believed that I had achieved the impossible, that through the power of diplomacy and goodwill, I had averted the catastrophe that loomed on the horizon.

But how naive I was, how blinded by my own optimism and the desperate desire to spare my people the horrors of another global conflagration. I see now, with the clarity of hindsight, that my efforts to placate the Nazi regime were nothing more than a fool's errand, a doomed attempt to reason with a madman consumed by dreams of conquest and domination.

I think of the Czechoslovakians, that proud and innocent people, whose sovereignty I so carelessly bartered away in the name of peace. The image of their crestfallen faces, the resignation and betrayal etched in every line, haunts me still, a searing reminder of the human cost of my misguided policies.

And then, the final, shattering blow—the invasion of Poland, the spark that ignited the powder keg of Europe and plunged the world into the abyss of war. As the tanks rolled across the border and the bombs rained down upon the cities, I felt the full weight of my failure come crashing down upon me, the realization that my best efforts had been nothing more than a prelude to the very catastrophe I had sought to prevent.

In the dark hours of the night, when sleep eludes me and the ghosts of the past come calling, I am tormented by the thought of what might have been, the lives that could have been saved, the suffering that could have been averted, had I only possessed the courage to stand firm against the forces of aggression.

I think of the brave men and women who took up arms in defense of freedom, the valiant souls who laid down their lives on the beaches of Dunkirk and the fields of France, the unsung heroes who endured the blitz and the privations of war with unbreakable spirit. How many of them, I wonder, cursed my name as they huddled in the rubble of their shattered homes, the victims of a war that I had failed to prevent?

And yet, even in the depths of my despair, I cannot help but cling to the belief that my intentions, however misguided, were born of a genuine desire for peace, a fervent hope that reason and diplomacy could triumph over the forces of hatred and division.

I think of the legacy I leave behind, the judgment of history that will forever brand me as the man who appeased the Nazis, the prime minister who failed to recognize the true nature of the threat that lurked beyond our shores. It is a burden I must bear, the price of my own naivete and the stubborn belief in the goodness of men.

But perhaps, in the end, there is a lesson to be learned from my story, a cautionary tale for those who would seek to appease the forces of tyranny and oppression. For the true path to peace lies not in the avoidance of conflict at all costs, but in the willingness to confront evil head-on, to stand firm in the face of aggression and defend the values that define us as a people.

As I sit here, the twilight of my life closing in around me, I offer a prayer for the world that I leave behind, a fervent hope that the hard-earned lessons of the war will not be forgotten. May those who come after me possess the wisdom and the courage to build a future free from the scourge of war, a world in which the voices of reason and compassion will always triumph over the drumbeat of hatred and intolerance.

And though my own part in this great drama may be nearing its end, I take solace in the knowledge that the indomitable spirit of my people, the resilience and fortitude that saw us through the darkest days of the war, will endure long after I am gone, a shining beacon of hope in a world that is all too often consumed by darkness.

For in the final accounting, it is not the mistakes we make that define us, but the courage and the grace with which we confront them, the determination to learn from the past and build a better future for all. And it is in this spirit that I offer my own story, a humble reminder of the frailty of human judgment and the enduring power of the human spirit.

May God bless and keep all those who have suffered and sacrificed in the cause of freedom, and may He grant us the strength and the wisdom to build a world worthy of their memory. For only by learning from the failures of the past can we hope to secure the peace and prosperity of generations yet to come.

# Chapter 42
# George Orwell
# The Weight of Words

As I lie here, the specter of death looming over me, I, George Orwell, find myself reflecting on the choices that have defined my life and the legacy I leave behind. The pen, once my sword and shield in the battle against tyranny and oppression, now feels heavy in my hand, weighted down by the burden of my own doubts and regrets.

I think back to the early days of my writing career, when the world seemed a simpler place, and the lines between right and wrong were starkly drawn. I had seen firsthand the brutality and injustice of imperialism during my time as a colonial policeman in Burma, and I had vowed to use my words to expose the ugly truths that lurked beneath the veneer of civilization.

But as the years passed and the political landscape grew ever more complex, I found myself grappling with the realization that the truth is rarely pure and never simple. The rise of totalitari-anism, the spread of propaganda, the erosion of individual liberty—these were the specters that haunted my waking hours and fueled my darkest nightmares.

In my quest to warn the world of the dangers that threatened to engulf us, I poured my heart and soul into my writing. From the dystopian nightmare of "1984" to the allegorical uprising of "Animal Farm," I sought to hold a mirror up to society, to force my readers to confront the harsh realities of power and control.

But even as my works found their audience and my name became synonymous with political dissent, I could not shake the feeling that I had somehow fallen short, that my words had not been enough to stem the tide of authoritarianism that seemed to be sweeping the world.

I think of the Spanish Civil War, where I fought alongside the socialist militia, determined to defend the cause of democracy against the forces of fascism. I remember the sense of camaraderie and purpose that filled my heart, the belief that we were part of a greater struggle for justice and freedom.

But I also remember the bitter taste of defeat, the crushing realization that our ideals had been no match for the ruthless efficiency of Franco's armies. And I think of the way my own experiences were later twisted and distorted by those who sought to use them for their own political ends, the way my name became a symbol of disillusionment and betrayal.

Perhaps my greatest regret is not the stances I took or the causes I championed, but the way in which my own certainty and conviction sometimes blinded me to the complexities of the world around me. I was so focused on the big picture, on the grand narratives of history and ideology, that I often failed to see the human stories that were unfolding before my very eyes.

I think of the people I met during my travels and my reporting, the ordinary men and women whose lives were shaped by forces beyond their control. The coal miners of northern England, the slum dwellers of Paris, the homeless and destitute of London—these were the people whose struggles and hopes and dreams I sought to capture in my writing.

But even as I gave voice to their experiences, I could not help but feel a sense of detachment, a nagging awareness of my own privilege and position. I was an observer, a chronicler of other people's lives, but I was not truly one of them. And in my quest to tell the truth as I saw it, I sometimes forgot to listen to the truths that others had to tell.

As I look back on my life and my work, I am struck by the weight of responsibility that comes with the written word. To write is to wield a kind of power, to shape the way people see themselves and the world around them. And with that power comes a duty to use it wisely, to strive for honesty and empathy in equal measure.

I cannot claim to have always lived up to that ideal, to have always found the perfect balance between passion and perspective. But I have tried, in my own imperfect way, to shine a light on the darkest corners of the human experience, to give voice to the voiceless and to speak truth to power.

Though my own journey may be nearing its end, my words will endure, serving as a testament to the enduring power of language and the vital role of the writer in society. Future generations will continue to grapple with the questions and challenges that I sought to address, building upon the foundation laid by those who came before.

For a writer's true legacy is measured not by fame or accolades, but by the impact of their words on the collective consciousness. It is the ideas that take root, the perspectives that shift, and the dialogues that are sparked that ultimately define the value of a literary life.

My regrets serve as a reminder of the weighty responsibility borne by those who wield the pen. May my words, imperfect as they may be, inspire others to take up the mantle of truth-telling, to fearlessly confront the complexities of our world, and to never stop fighting for a more just and equitable future.

# Chapter 43

# Gustav Klimt

## Pigments of Pain, Portraits of Loss

From the ethereal realms beyond the veil of mortal life, I, Gustav Klimt, gaze upon the world that endures long after my earthly days have drawn to a close. As I witness the unfolding tapestry of history, I find myself consumed by a profound sense of loss and regret, a haunting awareness of the fragility of art in the face of human cruelty and destruction.

I think of the collectors and patrons who once cherished my works, the kindred spirits who found in my paintings a reflection of their own deepest longings and dreams. How many of them, I wonder, were forced to surrender their beloved treasures to the insatiable hunger of the Third Reich, their lives upended and their hearts broken by the brutality of a regime that sought to extinguish the very light of creativity?

I remember the faces of those who sat for my portraits, the women whose essence I sought to capture with each stroke of my brush. Adele Bloch-Bauer, her countenance radiant with the enigmatic grace of the eternal feminine, her portrait a testament to the indomitable spirit of a people so long oppressed. The thought of her image, torn from the hands of those who loved her most, fills me with a profound sense of sorrow and loss.

And what of the countless other works, the luminous landscapes and mythic visions that sprang from the depths of my imagination? How many of them were lost to the flames of war, consigned to oblivion by the same hands that sought to erase the very memory of an entire people? The weight of those losses, the knowledge of the beauty that was forever stolen from the world, is a burden that I carry with me even in this ethereal realm.

And yet, even as I grapple with the pain of this shattered legacy, I find solace in the enduring power of art itself, the way in which a single image, a fleeting moment of revelation, can transcend the boundaries of time and space, speaking to the deepest truths of the human experience. I think of the works that survived, the paintings that emerged from the shadows of history to bear witness to the resilience of the human spirit, their colors still vibrant, their truths still resonant.

I take comfort in the knowledge that, despite the best efforts of those who sought to destroy them, my creations live on, continuing to inspire and move those who encounter them. In the stories of those who fought to reclaim what was lost, the descendants and advocates who refused to let the memory of these treasures fade away, I find a glimmer of hope amidst the darkness of history.

As I contemplate the mosaic of my life's work from this celestial vantage point, the shards of a legacy shattered by the forces of hatred and destruction, I am filled with a bittersweet mix of sorrow and gratitude. Sorrow for all that was lost, for the beauty that was so cruelly ripped away from the world, and gratitude for that which endures, for the unbreakable spirit of creation that lives on in the hearts and minds of those who continue to find meaning and inspiration in my work.

It is my hope that, as the years continue to unfold, my paintings will serve not only as a reminder of the beauty and passion that I poured into them, but also as a testament to the resilience of the human spirit, to the power of art to transcend even the darkest chapters of our history. May those who encounter my work find in it a source of solace, of healing, and of hope, a reminder that even in the face of the most unspeakable horrors, the light of creativity and beauty can never be fully extinguished.

# Chapter 44

# Pablo Picasso

## The Haunting Legacy of Guernica

The canvas looms large, a monstrous testament to the horrors of war. It is Guernica, my most famous work, a visceral depiction of the bombing of a Basque town during the Spanish Civil War. Its stark black, white, and grey figures writhe in agony, their distorted forms a symphony of pain and suffering.

It is a masterpiece, a powerful indictment of the brutality of war. Yet, as I stand before it, a wave of unease washes over me. I see the terror in the eyes of the victims, the anguish of the mothers clutching their dead children, the sheer futility of resistance in the face of overwhelming force.

But beyond the visceral impact of the painting, a deeper regret gnaws at me. Did I truly capture the essence of the tragedy? Did I do justice to the suffering of the people of Guernica?

I am haunted by the thought that my art, for all its power and raw emotion, is ultimately a pale imitation of reality. It can evoke empathy, outrage, and sorrow, but it cannot undo the damage, cannot bring back the dead, cannot heal the wounds of war.

I had hoped that Guernica would be a rallying cry for peace, a stark reminder of the consequences of violence. But as the world descends into another global conflict, I fear that my message has fallen on deaf ears.

The horrors of Guernica are replicated on a global scale, with millions more lives lost, countless cities reduced to rubble. The specter of war looms large, a dark cloud that threatens to engulf humanity in its destructive embrace.

I regret that my art has not been enough to prevent this madness, to awaken the world to the futility of violence. I regret that Guernica has become a symbol of human suffering, rather than a catalyst for peace.

But perhaps my greatest regret is the realization that my art, for all its power and influence, is ultimately powerless to change the course of history. It can reflect the darkness of the human heart, but it cannot erase it. It can expose the horrors of war, but it cannot prevent them.

As I stand before Guernica, a profound sense of humility washes over me. I am but a painter, a chronicler of the human condition. My art is a mirror, reflecting the beauty and ugliness of the world. But it is not a weapon, not a shield against the forces of destruction.

Perhaps my legacy will not be one of peace, but one of witness. A testament to the enduring power of art to bear witness to the horrors of war, to give voice to the voiceless, to remind us of our shared humanity.

And perhaps, in the end, that is enough. For in the face of darkness, even a flicker of light can offer hope, a glimmer of possibility that one day, we may learn to live in peace.

# Chapter 45

# Emperor Hirohito

## Lament for a Broken Pearl

 The Imperial Palace stands silent now, a gilded cage where echoes of the past linger in every corridor. The moon casts its pale glow upon the meticulously tended gardens, a serene facade that masks the turmoil within my heart. I am a prisoner of my own making, bound by tradition and duty, a puppet emperor with bloodstained hands.

I remember that fateful day, December 7th, 1941. The news of the attack on Pearl Harbor reached me like a thunderclap, shattering the illusion of peace. A day that would forever change the course of history, a day that would forever haunt my conscience.

I had been kept in the dark, a mere figurehead manipulated by the militarists who held the reins of power. They spoke of glory, of expanding the empire, of securing our rightful place in the world. I, blinded by my own naiveté and the weight of tradition, acquiesced to their demands.

But as the reports of the devastation poured in, the truth became clear. The attack on Pearl Harbor was not a glorious victory, but a catastrophic blunder. It unleashed a war that would consume millions of lives, including countless of my own subjects.

I saw the photographs of the burning ships, the mangled bodies of sailors, the terrified faces of civilians caught in the crossfire. The images seared into my soul, a constant reminder of the devastation wrought in my name.

In the years that followed, the war machine I had helped unleash ravaged Asia, leaving a trail of destruction and suffering in its wake. The atrocities committed by my soldiers, the horrors inflicted upon innocent civilians, filled me with shame and despair.

I tried to assert my authority, to reign in the warmongers, but it was too late. The war had taken on a life of its own, a monstrous entity fueled by hatred and ambition. I was powerless to stop it, a mere spectator to the unfolding tragedy.

And now, as the war ends in the ashes of Hiroshima and Nagasaki, I am left to grapple with the consequences of my actions. The weight of guilt is a heavy burden, one that I will carry with me to my grave.

I have been called a war criminal, a puppet of the militarists. Perhaps they are right. But I am also a man, a human being who grieves for the lives lost, who mourns the destruction of my country, who longs for a peaceful future.

In the quiet of the night, as the moon casts its ghostly glow upon the palace walls, I am haunted by the echoes of Pearl Harbor. The cries of the dying, the roar of the explosions, the silent tears of a nation plunged into darkness.

I regret my inaction, my failure to stand up to the warmongers, my complicity in the suffering of millions. I wish I could turn back time, undo the mistakes of the past, rewrite the history that has been written in blood.

But I cannot. All I can do is bear the burden of my guilt, strive for reconciliation, and pray that the lessons of the past will not be forgotten. For the sake of future generations, for the sake of humanity, we must never repeat the mistakes that led to the horrors of war.

# Chapter 46

# Franklin Delano Roosevelt

## Reflections on a National Disgrace

The weight of a nation rests upon my shoulders as I sit in the Oval Office, the world map sprawled before me. The United States, a beacon of hope and freedom, now finds itself engulfed in the darkness of war, a conflict that threatens to reshape the very fabric of our society.

I am Franklin D. Roosevelt, the 32nd President of the United States. It is a position I have held through the trials of the Great Depression and now, the crucible of World War II. The decisions I make in this room will echo through history, shaping the lives of millions and the destiny of nations.

And yet, as I reflect on my tenure, there is one decision that haunts me, a choice born of fear and prejudice, a stain upon the legacy I have fought so hard to build. The internment of Japanese Americans, the forced relocation and incarceration of over 120,000 innocent men, women, and children, is a burden I will carry to my grave.

I think back to the days following the attack on Pearl Harbor, the panic and rage that swept the nation. The cries for retribution, the fear of further attacks, the suspicion cast upon those of Japanese descent. In that moment, it seemed like a necessary evil, a way to protect the homeland from the threat of sabotage and espionage.

But as the war dragged on and the true scope of the internment became clear, I began to question the wisdom of my decision. The loyalty of Japanese Americans, the sacrifices they made for their country, the young men who fought and died under our flag—all of these truths stood in stark contrast to the fear and bigotry that drove our policies.

I think of the families torn apart, the lives uprooted, the dreams shattered. The Nisei soldiers, fighting for freedom abroad while their loved ones languished behind barbed wire at home. The economic losses, the mental anguish, the scars that would endure long after the last camp closed its gates.

In my darkest moments, I wonder how I could have let this happen, how I could have succumbed to the very prejudices we were fighting against. The Constitution, the bedrock of our democracy, was meant to protect the rights of all Americans, regardless of race or ancestry. And yet, in the name of national security, we trampled upon those very principles.

I think of the apologies and reparations that would come decades later, the acknowledgment of the wrongs committed. But for those who suffered, for those whose lives were forever altered, no amount of compensation could erase the pain and trauma endured.

As I near the end of my presidency and my life, I am haunted by the realization that even the most well-intentioned leaders can be led astray by fear and prejudice. The internment of Japanese Americans will forever remain a blight on our nation's history, a reminder of the fragility of our ideals in the face of adversity.

But perhaps, in confronting this painful chapter, we can find the strength to build a better future, to reaffirm our commitment to the values of equality, justice, and freedom for all. For it is only by acknowledging our mistakes, by learning from the darkest moments of our past, that we can hope to create a more perfect union.

And so, I leave this world with a heavy heart, but also with a glimmer of hope. The arc of the moral universe is long, but it bends toward justice. Let us work to ensure that the mistakes of the past are never repeated, that the sacrifices of those who suffered are not forgotten, and that the promise of America, the dream of a nation where all are created equal, is one day fully realized.

# Chapter 47
# Winston Churchill
## Quietude Denied

A shadow falls across my easel, and I don't need to turn to know there's a glass of brandy warming in those familiar hands.

"Penny for your thoughts, Winston?" Clementine's voice is a gentle brushstroke across a canvas already crowded with turbulent colors.

I sigh, laying down my brush. It has been a lifetime since we battled those early, brutal years together. Years where every dawn held the potential for disaster, every battle fought was etched, not on a map, but upon the landscape of my soul. I look upon the unfinished painting, a scene from those very days, and find something vital is absent.

"Clemmy," I begin, the familiar endearment rough and unused, "there is something... something missing."

Her silence is patient, a quiet canvas in this cluttered studio that has seen both triumph and frustration upon its walls.

"Don't mistake this for regret, my dearest," I clarify, words tumbling out as they so rarely do. "My life, it has been a whirlwind. I've walked with kings, painted with passion, and wielded words like swords across battlefields of both war and politics."

She sets the brandy down, and her touch on my shoulder is a weight I've known since those heady days when I was a mere lieutenant and she, a beauty who chose a soldier's uneven path over smoother avenues.

"Then this 'missing' thing, Winston, it cannot be any grand achievement. You, of all people, don't lack for trophies or renown."

"No, perhaps not," I concede, and yet a nagging itch lingers within me. Like a splinter that refuses to surface, it gnaws. It isn't fame I crave, nor another fight. My canvas, once alive with battleships and smoky skies, now begs me to render the olive groves of Chartwell or a serene sunset over Morocco.

"It is...simplicity, Clemmy. The quietude of the ordinary." I trace my own reflection in the drying paint. It's a grotesque thing, that portrait—a caricature of the bulldog the world knows, yet the aching hollowness in those eyes...that's the truth only a half-finished work can reveal.

"To have woken not to the clatter of dispatches and the ticking of some political timebomb," I muse, "but to birdsong and the scent of your roses. To fight no wars but the ones against weeds in the garden."

Her laugh is like cut crystal. "So, what stopped you, you silly man? There were long stretches of peace. We built a life at Chartwell."

"Not a true life, not with those shadows always at my shoulder. I was a statesman, a painter, a warhorse—never simply...a husband. Or a father. Always, there was England. Always, there was some crisis, a battle to be won."

"You make it sound like a curse."

"In some ways it was. A magnificent one, mind you," I hurry to add. "But those quiet minutes...they were stolen from me, devoured by a relentless hunger to do, to be." I turn from the painting, from that hollow-eyed glare. "Perhaps if I had painted more and politicked less..."

I trail off, for how can I ask for a different life, when the one I led shaped the very world before us? And yet, perhaps amongst those towering victories and those earth-shattering speeches, the greatest casualty was a simple life. A life of painting in the afternoon sun, of laughter with grandchildren, of a hand clasped in mine not to steady my resolve, but merely for the warmth of the familiar.

# Chapter 48
# Albert Einstein
# The Equation of Regret

The chalk dust lingers in the air, a ghostly reminder of equations and theories scribbled across the blackboard. I watch it settle, a slow dance of particles in the sunlight filtering through my study window. A lifetime's worth of scribbles, each one a testament to the relentless pursuit of knowledge.

Yet, in this quiet moment, surrounded by the tools of my trade, I find myself grappling with a different kind of equation. One that doesn't involve numbers or symbols, but the weight of choices and their consequences.

The letter sits on my desk, a stark reminder of the crossroads I once faced. A plea to President Roosevelt, urging the development of a weapon that could end a war, but at what cost? I had believed, naively perhaps, that it was a necessary evil. A means to an end, a way to stop a madman's reign of terror.

But now, the images of Hiroshima and Nagasaki haunt my dreams. The mushroom cloud, a grotesque mockery of the elegant equations that govern the universe. The silent screams of the victims, forever etched in my mind.

I had unlocked the secrets of the atom, but in doing so, I had unleashed a force that could destroy us all. The power of $E=mc^2$, once a source of intellectual wonder, now a terrifying specter.

I am a scientist, a seeker of truth. Yet, I find myself wrestling with the moral implications of my discoveries. Can knowledge, in and of itself, be evil? Or is it the application of that knowledge that determines its impact?

I had hoped that my work would illuminate the world, bring understanding and enlightenment. Instead, it cast a shadow, a chilling reminder of the destructive potential that lies within us all.

Perhaps my greatest regret is not the letter itself, but the naive belief that science exists in a vacuum. That it is immune to the forces of politics, war, and human ambition. I had underestimated the darkness that lurks in the hearts of men, the willingness to wield power for destruction.

I am not a religious man, but in this moment of quiet contemplation, I find myself seeking solace in the words of the Talmud: "Who is wise? One who foresees the consequences."

I had not foreseen the consequences. I had not anticipated the horrors that would be unleashed by my discoveries. And for that, I bear a burden of guilt that no amount of scientific accolades can erase.

Perhaps the true test of wisdom lies not in the pursuit of knowledge, but in the understanding of its potential for both good and evil. In the recognition that even the most brilliant minds can be blinded by ambition and fear.

As the chalk dust settles, I am left with a profound sense of humility. A reminder that even the most brilliant equations cannot solve the complex problems of human existence. That the pursuit of knowledge must always be tempered by wisdom, compassion, and a deep respect for the consequences of our actions.

# Chapter 49

# J. Robert Oppenheimer

## The Destroyer of Worlds

As I stand amidst the swirling sands of the Trinity test site, the weight of my creation bearing down upon my soul, I, J. Robert Oppenheimer, find myself lost in a labyrinth of regret and doubt. The brilliant flash of the atomic bomb, the searing heat that scorched the desert sky—these are the indelible marks of my legacy, the burdens I shall carry to my grave.

In the heady days of the Manhattan Project, we were driven by a sense of urgency and purpose, a conviction that our work would be the salvation of the free world. The specter of Nazi Germany loomed large, and we believed that the power of the atom was the only way to ensure the survival of democracy and freedom.

But now, as I sift through the ashes of Hiroshima and Nagasaki, as I hear the anguished cries of the innocent lives snuffed out in an instant, I am confronted by the horrifying realization that we had unleashed a force beyond our control, a promethean flame that threatens to consume us all.

The words of the Bhagavad Gita haunt me, a ghostly refrain that echoes through the corridors of my consciousness: "Now I am become Death, the destroyer of worlds." In the moment of the Trinity test, as I witnessed the awesome power of the bomb, I thought I understood the profound truth of those ancient words. But only now, in the aftermath of destruction and sorrow, do I truly comprehend their terrible significance.

I am plagued by doubts, by the nagging feeling that in our relentless pursuit of scientific knowledge, we had forgotten the fundamental wisdom of the Upanishads: "The Self is all this. Whoever sees all beings in the Self, and the Self in all beings, hates none." Did we, in our arrogance and hubris, lose sight of the essential unity of all things, the delicate web of life that binds us all together?

As I wander through the halls of academia, a once-celebrated physicist now haunted by the ghosts of his own creation, I seek solace in the timeless truths of Hinduism. The doctrine of karma, the eternal cycle of cause and effect, weighs heavily upon my mind. How many lifetimes will it take to balance the scales, to atone for the suffering we have wrought?

And yet, even as I grapple with the moral consequences of my work, I cannot help but feel a sense of awe at the scientific breakthroughs we achieved. The harnessing of the atom, the unlocking of the fundamental building blocks of the universe—these are the triumphs that will forever define my legacy, the gifts and the curses of a mind that dared to pierce the veil of the unknown.

But as I reflect on the long arc of my life, from the bright-eyed young physicist to the world-weary architect of destruction, I am struck by the realization that the true measure of our worth lies not in the brilliance of our intellects or the grandeur of our achievements, but in the wisdom and compassion with which we wield the power we have been given.

It is a lesson I learned too late, a truth that was obscured by the blinding light of the bomb. But as I stand here, in the twilight of my days, I can only hope that future generations will learn from our mistakes, that they will approach the awesome responsibility of scientific discovery with humility and reverence for the sanctity of life.

For in the end, we are all mere custodians of this fragile world, stewards of the precious gift of existence. And it is only by recognizing our shared humanity, by seeing ourselves in all beings and all beings in ourselves, that we can hope to build a future free from the specter of annihilation.

Let the story of my life, the cautionary tale of J. Robert Oppenheimer, be a reminder of the terrible price of unchecked power, the heavy burden of knowledge wielded without wisdom. And let us all strive to be the creators, not the destroyers, of worlds—to use our gifts in the service of life, in the pursuit of a brighter tomorrow for all who share this precious earth.

# Chapter 50

# Lord Mountbatten

## Midnight Specter of Partition

The grand halls of Viceroy's House stand silent now, a hollow echo of the bustling heart of empire it once was. Moonlight spills through the arched windows, casting long shadows that dance with the ghosts of decisions past. I pace the marble floors, a restless specter in this mausoleum of memory.

It was in these very rooms that the fate of a subcontinent was decided. Maps spread across the polished table, lines drawn and redrawn, carving up a nation like a butcher's prize. I, the last Viceroy of India, tasked with the impossible mission of granting independence while preserving peace.

Yet, as the clock ticked down to the fateful hour of Partition, the specter of violence loomed large. Reports poured in of communal clashes, of fear and hatred festering in the hearts of millions. I knew, deep down, that the lines we drew on paper would be etched in blood.

But there was no other way. The communal divide was too deep, the demands for separate nations too fervent. To delay independence would be to invite chaos, a bloodbath that could engulf the entire subcontinent.

So, with a heavy heart and a trembling hand, I signed the order that would tear India asunder. Two nations born from the ashes of empire, but at what cost?

The horrors that followed haunt my dreams. Millions displaced, families torn apart, violence erupting with a ferocity that shocked the world. The rivers ran red, the land stained with the blood of innocents.

I am haunted by the faces of those who suffered. The terrified eyes of refugees fleeing their homes, the anguished cries of mothers mourning their children, the silent despair of those who lost everything.

They say I am the architect of Partition, the man who divided a nation. But I was merely a pawn in a larger game, a puppet manipulated by forces beyond my control.

Yet, the guilt remains. The knowledge that my actions, however well-intentioned, unleashed a maelstrom of suffering. The regret that I could not find a way to bridge the divide, to forge a united India that could stand as a beacon of hope in a troubled world.

I wander the empty halls, a ghost among ghosts. The moonlight illuminates the portraits of my predecessors, their stern gazes seeming to judge my every move. They were architects of empire, builders of nations. I am the destroyer, the one who oversaw its unraveling.

The weight of history bears down on me, crushing my spirit. I am a man haunted by the past, tormented by the specter of what might have been.

Perhaps one day, history will judge me kindly. Perhaps it will recognize the impossible choices I faced, the sacrifices I made in the hope of averting a greater catastrophe.

But for now, I am left with the cold comfort of regret, a constant companion in the twilight of my life. The echoes of Partition will forever ring in my ears, a reminder of the fragility of peace and the enduring power of human folly.

# Chapter 51

# Mahatma Gandhi

# The Salt of Sorrow

The spinning wheel whispers its rhythmic tale as I guide the thread, each rotation a meditation on the path that led me here. The fabric of a nation, once woven with the threads of unity, now torn asunder by the very hands that sought to set it free.

I close my eyes and see the faces of those who suffered, those who lost their lives in the chaos of Partition. The weight of their suffering hangs heavy on my soul, a burden I bear with each breath.

I had dreamed of an India united, a tapestry of faiths and cultures, each thread contributing to the beauty of the whole. But in the end, the pull of division proved stronger than the bonds of unity.

As I sit here, the Partition looms like a specter, a haunting reminder of the fragility of peace and the consequences of our actions. The lines drawn on maps, the borders that now separate brother from brother, sister from sister.

I cannot help but question the path I chose, the principles of non-violence and satyagraha that guided my every step. Did I do enough to prevent this fracturing? Could I have been more forceful in my opposition to the divisions that now scar the soul of our nation?

The salt of the earth, once a symbol of our defiance against oppression, now tastes bitter on my tongue. The wounds of Partition, still fresh and raw, serve as a reminder of the price we paid for our freedom.

I think of the countless lives uprooted, the families torn apart by the tides of history. The refugee camps, the stories of loss and despair, each one a searing indictment of the failures of leadership.

In my quest for independence, had I forgotten the true essence of swaraj? The self-rule that begins within, the mastery over one's own passions and prejudices?

The Partition stands as a testament to the dangers of division, the perils of allowing our differences to define us. It is a lesson that we must learn, a wound that we must heal, if we are to move forward as a nation.

As I spin the wheel, each thread a prayer for unity, I am reminded of the power of forgiveness, the necessity of compassion in the face of adversity. The path ahead may be uncertain, but I hold fast to the belief that the spirit of ahimsa, the force of non-violence, can still be a guiding light in the darkness.

For in the end, it is not the borders that define us, but the humanity that resides within each of us. It is the recognition of our shared struggles, our common hopes and dreams, that will ultimately bind us together.

The Partition may be my greatest regret, but it is also a call to action, a reminder of the work that remains unfinished. The true swaraj, the freedom that comes from within, is still a distant dream.

But I will continue to spin the wheel, to weave the threads of unity, until my last breath. For in the tapestry of India, each thread, each life, is sacred and worthy of love.

# Chapter 52
# George Foreman
## The Heavyweight of Hubris

The roar of the crowd, the heat of the African night, the glare of the spotlights—it all comes rushing back to me like a fevered dream, a moment frozen in time. I, George Foreman, the undefeated heavyweight champion of the world, stood in the center of the ring, my fists raised in anticipation of the glory that was sure to be mine. Across from me, Muhammad Ali, the deposed king, the man I was destined to dethrone once and for all.

But fate, it seems, had a different plan in store for me that night in Kinshasa. As the bell rang and the fight began, I charged forward with all the power and fury of a man possessed, raining down blows upon Ali like a relentless storm. I was sure that victory was mine, that no man could withstand the force of my onslaught.

And yet, as the rounds ticked by and my arms grew heavy with fatigue, I began to realize the folly of my own arrogance. Ali, the wily old fox, had lured me into a trap of his own making, absorbing my punches like a sponge and waiting for me to exhaust myself against the ropes. The "Rope-a-Dope," they would call it later—a stroke of tactical genius that would go down in history as one of the greatest feats of boxing brilliance ever seen.

But in that moment, as I felt my strength ebbing away and saw the gleam of triumph in Ali's eyes, all I could feel was the crushing weight of my own hubris. I had underestimated my opponent, had failed to see the cunning behind his seemingly passive approach. And now, as he unleashed a barrage of precise, stinging blows that sent me reeling, I knew that I had been outfoxed, outmaneuvered, and outfought by a true master of the game.

The final blow, a right hook that crumpled me to the canvas, was almost a mercy. As I lay there, the referee counting down the seconds of my defeat, I felt a sense of shock and disbelief wash over me. I, George Foreman, the man who had been deemed unbeatable, had been humbled in front of the entire world.

In the weeks and months that followed, as the magnitude of my loss sank in and the headlines trumpeted Ali's incredible comeback, I was forced to confront the depths of my own regret. I had let my own ego blind me to the realities of the fight, had failed to adapt to the changing circumstances of the battle. And in doing so, I had not only lost the match, but had also lost a piece of myself, the aura of invincibility that had been my shield and my sword.

It took me years to come to terms with the lessons of that night, to realize that true greatness lies not in the absence of defeat, but in the ability to learn and grow from it. Ali had taught me, through the sting of his fists and the brilliance of his mind, that humility and adaptability are the keys to lasting success in the ring and in life.

And so, as I look back on that moment, that turning point in my journey as a fighter and a man, I am filled not only with the pain of regret, but also with a sense of gratitude. For it was in the crucible of that defeat that I was forced to confront my own limitations, to ask myself hard questions about who I was and what I stood for.

The "Rumble in the Jungle" will forever be remembered as Ali's greatest triumph, a shining example of the power of resilience and the indomitable nature of the human spirit. But for me, it will always be something more personal, more profound—a reminder of the perils of pride and the wisdom that can only be gained through the bitter taste of failure.

I may have lost the fight that night in Kinshasa, but in the long run, I gained something far more valuable—a deeper understanding of myself, a clearer vision of what truly matters in this fleeting dance we call life. And for that, I will always be grateful to the man who showed me the folly of my own conceit, the greatest of all time, Muhammad Ali.

# Chapter 53

# Lance Armstrong

# The Unraveling of the Yellow Jersey

In the solitude of my thoughts, far from the roaring crowds and the flash of cameras that once defined my every waking moment, I, Lance Armstrong, find myself confronted by the specter of a legacy forever tarnished by the choices I made. The yellow jerseys that once stood as a testament to my unparalleled dominance in the world of cycling now hang heavy with the weight of deception and regret.

I think back to the early days of my career, when the thrill of competition and the pursuit of excellence first took hold of my soul. I had always been a fighter, a man possessed by an unquenchable thirst to be the best, to push myself beyond the limits of what seemed humanly possible. And in the grueling world of professional cycling, I found the ultimate canvas upon which to paint the masterpiece of my ambition.

But as the years passed and the pressures mounted, as the expectations of fans and sponsors alike grew ever more suffocating, I found myself drawn into a web of deceit and moral compromise. The decision to use performance-enhancing drugs, to engage in the systematic doping that would come to define the darkest chapter of my life, was not made lightly. But in the heat of the moment, caught up in the relentless pursuit of victory at any cost, it seemed like the only path forward.

I told myself that everyone was doing it, that to compete at the highest levels of the sport meant embracing the unwritten rules of the game. I convinced myself that my talent, my work ethic, my sheer force of will would be enough to transcend the ethical quandaries that gnawed at the edges of my conscience. But as the deceptions piled up and the web of lies grew ever more tangled, I could feel the weight of my choices bearing down upon me like a crushing burden.

The day of reckoning, when the truth of my misdeeds finally came to light, was a moment of searing humiliation and soul-crushing regret. To stand before the world, stripped of my titles and my dignity, and admit to the depths of my own deception—it was a pain unlike any I had ever known, a wound that cut straight to the core of my being.

In the aftermath of the scandal, as I grappled with the ruins of my once-glorious reputation, I was forced to confront the true cost of my actions. The disappointment in the eyes of my children, the shame and anger of the fans who had once idolized me, the knowledge that my name would forever be synonymous with cheating and betrayal—these were the bitter fruits of a legacy poisoned by my own hubris and deceit.

And yet, even in the depths of my disgrace, I could not help but feel a flicker of defiance, a stubborn refusal to let my mistakes define the entirety of my being. For I knew that the journey that had brought me to the pinnacle of my sport, the countless hours of training and sacrifice, the battles waged against cancer and self-doubt—these were not the actions of a man without integrity, without a fundamental core of decency and strength.

In the years since my fall from grace, as I have sought to make amends and rebuild some semblance of a life beyond the shadow of my transgressions, I have come to understand the true meaning of redemption. It is not a matter of erasing the past, of pretending that the wrongs we have committed never happened. Rather, it is about facing our demons head-on, about taking responsibility for our actions and working every day to be a better version of ourselves.

For me, that has meant pouring my energy into the fight against cancer, into using my platform and my resources to make a difference in the lives of those battling the disease that once nearly claimed my own life. It has meant being a better father, a better friend, a better man—not in spite of my mistakes, but because of them, because of the hard-won wisdom and humility that can only be forged in the crucible of failure and regret.

And though I know that my legacy will forever be a complicated one, forever shadowed by the specter of my own misdeeds, I cling to the hope that in the end, the good that I have done, the lives that I have touched, will somehow outweigh the darkness of my past. For in the final analysis, we are all flawed creatures, all capable of great feats of courage and great acts of weakness. And it is only through the constant struggle to be better, to rise above our own shortcomings, that we can hope to leave this world a little bit brighter than we found it.

To those who once believed in me, who saw in my triumphs a reflection of their own hopes and dreams, I offer my deepest apologies and my most profound regrets. I am sorry for the pain that my actions caused, for the trust that I betrayed, for the legacy that

I so carelessly tarnished. And I vow to spend the rest of my days working to be worthy of the second chance that I have been given, to use my voice and my platform to make a positive difference in the world.

For in the end, the true measure of a life is not found in the victories we achieve or the accolades we accumulate, but in the way we respond to our own failures and shortcomings. It is in the quiet moments of reflection and the daily acts of courage and compassion that we find our true strength, our true purpose. And it is in the unwavering pursuit of that purpose, in the face of all obstacles and all regrets, that we can finally begin to write the story of a life well-lived.

# Chapter 54
# Fidel Castro
## The Revolution's Rust

The aroma of tobacco hangs heavy, a familiar ghost in this quiet office. There's a stack of papers beside my worn leather chair, reports on sugar rations, whispers of dissent in the provinces—petty distractions for a mind that once devoured maps and strategies. I push them aside, yearning for the simplicity of a cleaning rag and the warm gleam of a well-oiled rifle.

A lifetime ago, it seems. When the mountains were my cathedral, and the rustle of leaves my congregation. Those were the days, mis muchachos, when the fight burned pure, when the cause was a single gleaming star in the night sky. I was El Comandante, a hurricane harnessed into human form.

Now...now I am an old man grappling with ledgers and reports. The revolution, it seems, has a taste for bureaucracy.

I close my eyes, a flicker of those Sierra Maestra days playing before me. The camaraderie around a fire, the shared crust of bread, the thrill of danger just a valley away. It was a life lived on the edge, a constant dance with death and the intoxicating smell of cordite.

"Fidel?" A voice, soft as rain. Celia. Even now, the gentle strength in her eyes has the power to settle the storm in my soul. She, who walked beside me through it all, the truest believer.

"Merely reminiscing, mi amor," I murmur. There is a tiredness in me that no amount of sleep can cure. Is it age, or is it something more...amorphous?

She perches on the edge of my desk, and her touch is feather-light on my cheek. "Missing the fight, are you?"

I chuckle, the sound rough in my own ears. "Perhaps a little. Those were simpler times. Revolution was...well, revolutionary."

We both know the irony—of how the revolution we built ossified into something rigid, suspicious. The bright fervor of our ideals crusted over with the inevitable grime of power, of control. I was a soldier once, not a politician. The jungle, it held cleaner enemies than the smiles I'm forced to barter with now.

"Would you have done anything differently?" Celia asks. There is no accusation in her voice, only the weight of shared history.

I stare at my hands, gnarled and scarred from a lifetime of struggle. Did we give them paradise with a side of fear? Were our promises of equality swallowed whole by the monster of necessity?

"Every great venture leaves a trail of...debris," I say at last. "Some are fallen comrades along the road. Others...they are pieces of your own ideals, compromises you never thought you'd make."

I can't face her. I think of Che, his face frozen on a thousand t-shirts, a martyr to a cause he might not recognize now. I think of the farmers who bend their backs to meet quotas, the whispered jokes in darkened rooms, the intellectuals who once marched with us now choosing exile.

Perhaps the greatest casualty of a revolution is not the body count, but the slow bleed of the dream itself. We fought for freedom, yes, but freedom became a many-headed beast once we tried to tame it. My greatest battle wasn't against armies, but the creeping rot of absolute power. And in that fight, old friend, perhaps I was on the losing side.

# Chapter 55

# Che Guevara

# The Weight of the Guerilla's Beret

In the solitude of my final moments, as the echoes of the guerrilla struggle fade into the mists of memory, I, Ernesto "Che" Guevara, find myself reflecting on the winding path of my life as a revolutionary. The ideals that once burned so fiercely in my heart now feel like embers, glowing with a bittersweet intensity as I confront the reality of my own mortality.

I think back to the early days of the Cuban Revolution, when the promise of a new world order seemed within our grasp. Alongside my comrades-in-arms, I fought to overthrow the tyranny of the Batista regime, fueled by a belief in the power of the people to forge their own destiny. We were young, idealistic, and convinced that through the barrel of a gun, we could reshape society in the image of our socialist dreams.

But as the years passed and the challenges of building a new Cuba mounted, I began to feel the weight of the compromises and contradictions that came with the exercise of power. The very state apparatus that we had sought to dismantle became the instrument of our rule, and the dream of a classless society gave way to the realities of political expediency and economic hardship.

I grappled with the knowledge that the revolution I had fought for was not immune to the corrupting influence of power, that even the most noble of intentions could be twisted in the crucible of geopolitical struggle. The Soviet Union, once our ally and benefactor, sought to bend Cuba to its own will, and the dream of a truly independent socialist state seemed to slip further from our grasp.

And then there were the missions abroad, the attempts to export the revolution to other shores. From the Congo to Bolivia, I sought to ignite the flames of insurgency, to inspire the oppressed masses to rise up and claim their birthright. But in the jungles and mountains of foreign lands, I was forced to confront the limits of my own influence, the intractable realities of local politics and the indifference of a world that seemed content to watch from the sidelines.

Perhaps my greatest regret is the realization that the path of armed struggle, the very means by which we had achieved our own liberation, was not a panacea for the ills of the world. The violence and bloodshed, the sacrifices of the innocent and the guilty alike—these were the unavoidable costs of the revolutionary dream, the price that had to be paid for the promise of a better tomorrow.

And yet, even as I lay here, my body broken but my spirit undiminished, I cannot bring myself to renounce the ideals that have guided my life. The struggle for justice, for dignity, for the right of every human being to live free from the shackles of oppression—these are the things that I have fought for, the very essence of what it means to be a revolutionary.

My only hope is that the seeds of change that we have planted, the sparks of resistance that we have kindled, will continue to grow and spread, even in the face of adversity. The road ahead may be long and the obstacles many, but I have faith in the resilience and the determination of those who continue the fight, who refuse to accept the world as it is and dare to dream of a better future.

Let my legacy be not just the battles won or lost, but the enduring power of the revolutionary spirit to inspire and transform. And let my regrets serve as a reminder of the heavy burdens and terrible costs that come with the pursuit of radical change, the sacrifices that must be made in the name of a higher cause.

In the end, I go to my grave with the knowledge that I have given all that I had to give, that I have lived and died for something greater than myself. And though the world may judge me as it will, I can only hope that the flame of rebellion that I have carried within me will continue to burn, a beacon of hope for all those who struggle against the tyranny of injustice.

# Chapter 56
# Mao Zedong
## The Bitter Harvest of Revolution

In the heart of the Forbidden City, amidst the echoes of a nation's tumultuous past, I, Mao Zedong, the architect of a new China, sit alone with my thoughts, the weight of a lifetime's decisions bearing down upon me like the ancient stones of the palace walls.

I gaze out upon the vast expanse of Tiananmen Square, the place where I once stood as a young revolutionary, filled with the fire of idealism and the unshakable conviction that I could reshape the world in the image of my dreams. But now, as the twilight of my years approaches, I find myself haunted by the specter of unintended consequences, the bitter harvest of a revolution that has left my people reeling in its wake.

In my mind's eye, I see the faces of the millions who perished during the Great Leap Forward, the grand vision that became a nightmare of starvation and suffering. I had sought to propel

China into the future, to transform a backward agrarian society into a modern industrial powerhouse. But in my zeal to remake the world, I failed to heed the warnings of history, the lessons of human nature.

I thought I could bend the forces of economics to my will, that sheer determination and revolutionary fervor could overcome the immutable laws of supply and demand. But as the crops withered in the fields and the people starved in the streets, I began to realize the terrible price of my hubris, the folly of a man who thought himself above the wisdom of the ages.

And then came the Cultural Revolution, the great purge that was meant to cleanse the nation of its feudal past and forge a new socialist utopia. I had believed that by unleashing the fury of the masses, by encouraging the young to rise up against the old order, I could sweep away the vestiges of tradition and build a society based on the principles of Marxism-Leninism.

But what I unleashed was a tide of chaos and destruction, a frenzy of violence and persecution that tore at the very fabric of Chinese society. The Red Guards, the fanatical youth who worshipped me as a demigod, became a force of terror, destroying priceless cultural treasures, humiliating and brutalizing anyone deemed an enemy of the revolution.

I watched as loyal party members were denounced and purged, as intellectuals and artists were sent to labor camps, as families were torn apart and lives were shattered. And though I had once reveled in the adulation of the masses, though I had basked in the glow of my own cult of personality, I began to feel a creeping sense of unease, a gnawing doubt that perhaps I had unleashed forces beyond my control.

Now, as I sit in the twilight of my reign, I am haunted by the ghosts of my own making, the millions of lives sacrificed on the altar of my revolutionary vision. I think of the great famine, the cultural destruction, the reign of terror that marked the darkest chapters of my rule. And I cannot help but wonder if, in my quest to create a new China, I have instead sown the seeds of its undoing.

I had sought to liberate my people from the yoke of imperialism and feudalism, to give them a voice and a stake in their own destiny. But in my single-minded pursuit of that goal, I became a tyrant in my own right, a man who demanded unquestioning obedience and brook no dissent.

And yet, even as I grapple with the weight of my own mistakes, I cannot help but cling to the belief that the revolution was necessary, that the old order had to be swept away in order to build a new and better world. I think of the strides we have made, the great leaps forward in industry and agriculture, the sense of national pride and purpose that has been rekindled in the hearts of the Chinese people.

But at what cost? That is the question that haunts me now, the reckoning that I must face as I prepare to meet my maker. How many lives were sacrificed, how much suffering was endured, in the name of the greater good? And was it worth it, in the end?

These are the questions that I will take with me to the grave, the burdens that I must bear as the architect of a revolution that remade the world's most populous nation. I know that history will judge me harshly, that I will be remembered as much for my crimes as for my triumphs.

But perhaps that is the price of greatness, the inevitable consequence of daring to dream on such a grand scale. For in the end, the only true measure of a revolutionary is not the accolades of the present, but the judgment of posterity.

And so, I will face that judgment with the same unflinching resolve that has guided me through a lifetime of struggle and sacrifice. I will bear the weight of my mistakes, the bitter harvest of my revolutionary vision. And I will hope that, in the fullness of time, the Chinese people will find a way to build on the foundations that I have laid, to create a society that is truly just, truly equal, and truly free.

For that is the only legacy that matters, the only monument that will endure long after the last stone of the Forbidden City has crumbled to dust. And it is the only hope that sustains me now, as I confront the ghosts of my past and the uncertain verdict of history.

# Chapter 57

# Colonel Christian de Castries

## The Ghosts of Dien Bien Phu

In the haunted recesses of my memory, the specters of Dien Bien Phu loom large, their silent accusations echoing through the corridors of my conscience. I, Colonel Christian de Castries, once the proud commander of the French forces in that fateful valley, now find myself consumed by the bitter ashes of defeat, the weight of my own miscalculations bearing down upon my soul like a millstone.

The decision to establish a fortified base at Dien Bien Phu seemed like a stroke of strategic brilliance at the time, a way to cut off the Viet Minh's supply lines and strike a decisive blow against the communist insurgency. I believed that our superior firepower and tactical expertise would be more than a match for the ragtag guerrilla forces that opposed us, that the natural defenses of the valley would make our position all but impregnable.

But I, in my hubris and arrogance, failed to grasp the true nature of the enemy we faced. The Viet Minh, under the brilliant leadership of General Vo Nguyen Giap, proved far more resourceful and determined than I ever could have imagined. They hauled artillery pieces up the steep slopes of the surrounding mountains, dug intricate networks of tunnels and trenches, and launched wave after wave of relentless attacks against our beleaguered garrison.

As the battle raged on and our losses mounted, I found myself confronted with the harsh realities of command, the agonizing choices that must be made in the heat of combat. The decision to launch a counterattack, the allocation of dwindling resources, the cold calculus of prioritizing certain positions over others—each call weighed heavily upon my conscience, the lives of my men hanging in the balance.

And yet, even as I grappled with the tactical challenges of the moment, I couldn't shake the gnawing sense that the battle itself was a fundamentally flawed endeavor, a doomed attempt to prop up a crumbling colonial edifice. The Viet Minh, for all their ruthlessness and zeal, were fighting for a cause that resonated deeply with the Vietnamese people—the desire for self-determination, for freedom from foreign domination. What were we fighting for, in the end, but the preservation of an unjust and unsustainable status quo?

As the final days of the battle approached and our defeat became all but certain, I was haunted by the realization that my own failures of judgment and leadership had contributed to the unfolding catastrophe. The lives lost, the wounds suffered, the dreams shattered—all of it weighed upon my soul like a leaden shroud, a burden that I would carry with me for the rest of my days.

And then came the brutal denouement, the fall of Dien Bien Phu and the ignominious surrender of the French forces. As I watched the tricolour being lowered for the last time and the Viet Minh flag rising in its place, I felt a profound sense of shame and despair, a realization that my own actions had played a part in the unraveling of an empire and the birth of a new era in Southeast Asia.

The aftermath of the battle was a blur of recrimination and soul-searching, a reckoning with the consequences of our collective failure. The Geneva Accords, which partitioned Vietnam and set the stage for the American involvement in the region, seemed like a bitter epilogue to the tragedy of Dien Bien Phu, a reminder of the far-reaching impact of our defeat.

For me, the ghosts of that distant valley have never truly been laid to rest. The faces of the fallen, the echoes of their final moments, the weight of my own responsibility—these are the specters that haunt my waking hours and disturb my fitful sleep. I am left to grapple with the painful truth that my own shortcomings as a leader, my own inability to see beyond the narrow confines of my colonial mindset, contributed to a defeat that would shape the course of history.

As I reflect on the lessons of Dien Bien Phu, I am struck by the hubris and folly of those who would seek to impose their will upon others through force of arms. The Vietnam War, which grew out of the ashes of our failure, stands as a grim testament to the limits of military power and the enduring resilience of the human spirit in the face of oppression.

May the sacrifice of those who fought and died on both sides of that conflict serve as a sobering reminder of the true costs of war, and may we, as a species, learn to seek our common humanity in the pursuit of justice and self-determination. For only then can we hope to build a world where the tragedy of Dien Bien Phu is but a fading memory, a cautionary tale of the perils of empire and the enduring struggle for freedom.

# Chapter 58

# General William Westmoreland

## The Burden of an Unwinnable War

In the solitude of my study, far from the battlefields and command centers that once consumed my every waking moment, I, General William Westmoreland, find myself haunted by the specter of a war that defined my career and forever altered the course of a nation. As the commander of U.S. forces in Vietnam during the most pivotal years of that conflict, I bear a burden of responsibility and regret that time has done little to ease.

I think back to those early days, when the path to victory seemed clear and the might of the American military machine appeared invincible. I had faith in our strategy, in the belief that superior firepower and technology would ultimately break the will of the enemy and secure a decisive triumph for the cause of freedom.

But as the months turned to years and the casualty lists grew ever longer, I began to feel the gnawing sense that we were trapped in a quagmire of our own making.

I had underestimated the tenacity and adaptability of our foe, the depth of their commitment to their cause and their willingness to endure unimaginable hardships in pursuit of it. The North Vietnamese and Viet Cong forces proved far more resilient and tactically adept than we had anticipated, employing guerrilla warfare and political maneuvering to frustrate our every move. And yet, I clung to the belief that one more offensive, one more surge of troops and resources, would turn the tide and bring the enemy to their knees.

But as the war dragged on and the political and social fabric of our own nation began to fray, I found myself increasingly isolated and embattled. The strategy of attrition, of wearing down the enemy through sheer force of arms, had become a double-edged sword, leading to high American casualties and a growing sense of futility and despair among the troops. The body counts that I had relied upon as a measure of progress began to ring hollow, a grim reminder of the human cost of a war with no clear end in sight.

I think of the young men who fought and died under my command, the brave soldiers who sacrificed everything in service to their country. I see their faces in my dreams, hear their voices in the quiet moments of reflection. And I cannot escape the terrible knowledge that for all their courage and devotion, for all the blood and treasure we poured into that distant land, we were unable to achieve the victory they so deserved.

In my darkest moments, I am haunted by the thought that I failed them, that my own strategic miscalculations and stubbornness in the face of mounting evidence contributed to the prolonging of a war that might have been ended sooner, with fewer lives lost. The decisions I made, the orders I gave, the public statements

I made in defense of our mission—all of these weigh heavily upon my conscience, a burden that I will carry to my grave.

And yet, even as I grapple with the painful realities of Vietnam and my own role in its tragedy, I cannot help but feel a sense of pride in the men and women who served there, in their bravery and selflessness in the face of unimaginable adversity. They fought not for glory or conquest, but for each other and for the ideals that our nation holds dear. And though the war may have ended in stalemate and disillusionment, their courage and sacrifice will forever stand as a testament to the enduring spirit of the American soldier.

As I look back on those turbulent years, I am struck by the hard lessons that Vietnam taught us, the painful truths that we as a nation were forced to confront. The limits of military power, the dangers of hubris and overreach, the need for clear objectives and honest communication with the American people—these are the bitter fruits of a war that tested us to our very soul.

And yet, even as I acknowledge my own failings and the terrible price we paid for them, I cannot help but feel a sense of hope for the future. For if we can learn from the mistakes of Vietnam, if we can find the wisdom and the courage to chart a new course in our engagement with the world, then perhaps the sacrifices of those who fought and died there will not have been in vain.

Ultimately, the true legacy of Vietnam lies not in the battles won or lost, but in the hard-earned wisdom that we as a nation must carry forward. It lies in the recognition that war, for all its terrible necessity, must always be a last resort, and that the true measure of a great power lies not in its ability to impose its will through force of arms, but in its capacity for restraint, compassion, and the pursuit of a just and lasting peace.

These are the lessons that I carry with me, the regrets that I will bear for all my days. And though I may never fully escape the shadow of Vietnam, I take solace in the knowledge that its sacrifices and its sorrows have the power to reshape our understanding of war and our place in the world.

To the soldiers who fought under my command, to the families who lost loved ones in that distant conflict, I offer my deepest apologies and my eternal gratitude. Your bravery and your sacrifices will forever be remembered, even as we strive to build a future worthy of your courage and your devotion.

And to the American people, I offer this final reflection: let us never forget the hard lessons of Vietnam, the bitter wisdom bought at so high a price. Let us honor the memory of those who served by recommitting ourselves to the ideals of democracy, freedom, and human dignity that they fought and died to defend. And let us always strive to be a nation worthy of their sacrifice, a beacon of hope and justice in a troubled world.

# Chapter 59

# Lyndon Johnson

# The Specter of Vietnam

In the solitude of my own thoughts, I find myself haunted by the specter of a war that shattered my dreams and left an indelible scar upon my legacy. I, Lyndon Baines Johnson, the 36th President of the United States, bear the burden of a decision that would come to define not only my presidency but the very soul of our nation.

Vietnam. The word itself is a dagger in my heart, a reminder of the hubris and the folly that led me to believe that we could bend the course of history to our will. I had inherited this conflict, a tangled web of politics and ideology, and I made the fateful choice to escalate, to pour more blood and treasure into the jungles of Southeast Asia.

I believed, with every fiber of my being, that we were fighting for a just cause, that we could not allow the dominoes of communism to topple across the region. I listened to the voices of my advisors, the hawks who whispered promises of victory and the glory of American exceptionalism.

But as the war dragged on and the casualties mounted, as the protests grew louder and the divisions in our society turned to chasms, I began to feel the weight of my own miscalculation. I watched as the best and brightest of our nation's youth were sacrificed on the altar of a distant conflict, their lives cut short by the hubris of old men in suits.

I think of the mothers and fathers, the wives and children, who lost their loved ones in the jungles and the deltas of Vietnam. I think of the wounded, the scarred, the haunted, who came home to a nation that did not understand their sacrifice. And I am consumed by the knowledge that it was I who sent them there, I who bore the responsibility for their suffering.

In the depths of my regret, I am forced to confront the painful truth that my own pride and stubbornness blinded me to the reality of the situation. I refused to listen to the voices of dissent, the wise men who warned of the quagmire we were entering. I believed that American power and ingenuity could overcome any obstacle, that we could will our way to victory through sheer force of arms.

But Vietnam was a different kind of war, a conflict that could not be won by bombers and battalions alone. It was a war of hearts and minds, of ideologies and loyalties, and we were woefully unprepared for the complexities and the contradictions of this foreign land.

I think of the Great Society, the vision I had for a nation that would use its wealth and its power to lift up the poor and the marginalized. I think of the Civil Rights Act, the Voting Rights Act, the programs that were meant to build a more just and equitable America. And I am haunted by the knowledge that Vietnam sapped the energy and the resources that could have brought that dream to fruition.

In the end, it was the weight of my own conscience that forced me to confront the reality of my mistake. I could no longer justify the sacrifice of American lives for a cause that had lost its way. I could no longer bear the burden of a war that had torn our nation asunder.

And so, with a heavy heart, I made the decision not to seek re-election, to step aside and allow the country to heal from the wounds that I had inflicted. It was the hardest choice of my life, an admission of failure that went against every instinct of my political being.

But even as I retreated into the shadows, even as I watched the war drag on for years more, I knew that the stain of Vietnam would forever mar my legacy. I had sought to do what was right, to use American power as a force for good in the world. But in the end, I had only succeeded in leading us into a quagmire from which there was no easy escape.

This is my burden, the regret that I will carry with me to my grave. The knowledge that my decisions, my stubbornness, my pride, had cost so many lives and shattered so many dreams. The realization that in trying to save a distant land from communism, I had nearly torn my own nation apart.

I can only hope that future generations will learn from my mistakes, that they will understand the limits of American power and the dangers of hubris. That they will seek the wisdom to know when to fight and when to seek peace, when to stand firm and when to compromise.

For after all, the true measure of a leader is not in the battles won or the enemies vanquished, but in the lives uplifted and the dreams fulfilled. And on that score, I fear that my legacy will forever be shadowed by the specter of a war that I could not win, and a dream that I could not fully realize.

# Chapter 60

# F. W. de Klerk

## The Shadow of Apartheid

As I sit in the fading light of my office, the weight of history pressing down upon my shoulders, I, Frederik Willem de Klerk, the last State President of the apartheid era, find myself haunted by the specter of a past that cannot be undone. The decisions I made, the actions I took, the system I upheld—all of it now comes back to me in a rush of shame and regret, a reckoning that has been long in the making.

I think back to my early days in politics, a young man filled with the certainty and the arrogance of youth. I believed in the rightness of our cause, in the necessity of preserving white rule and the separation of the races. I climbed the ranks of the National Party, embracing the ideology of apartheid, convinced that it was the only path to stability and prosperity for our nation.

But even then, deep within my heart, I could feel the stirrings of doubt, the gnawing sense that the world we had built was founded on a lie. I saw the suffering in the eyes of the black South Africans, the degradation and the despair of a people denied their basic humanity. And though I tried to push these thoughts aside, to bury them beneath the weight of duty and loyalty, they never truly left me.

As the years passed and the cries for change grew louder, I found myself increasingly torn between the demands of my position and the dictates of my conscience. I watched as our country teetered on the brink of chaos, as the violence and the unrest threatened to tear us apart. And though I clung to the belief that apartheid could be reformed, that we could find a way to preserve white power while easing the plight of the black majority, I knew in my heart that it was a futile dream.

When I became State President in 1989, I knew that the time had come for a reckoning, for a brave new course that would lead our nation out of the darkness and into the light. I reached out to Nelson Mandela and the African National Congress, seeking to forge a new path of negotiation and compromise. And though the road was fraught with peril and resistance, though there were those who sought to derail our efforts at every turn, we pressed on, driven by the conviction that there was no other way.

But even as we worked to dismantle the structures of apartheid, to build a new and more just society, I could not escape the weight of my own guilt, the knowledge that I had been complicit in a system that had caused untold suffering and pain. I thought of the lives that had been lost, the families that had been torn apart, the dreams that had been shattered on the altar of white supremacy.

In the end, when the moment of truth arrived and I stood before the world to announce the end of apartheid, I felt a sense of relief and release, a burden lifted from my soul. But even then, I knew that the work of healing and reconciliation had only just begun, that the scars of the past would take generations to fade.

As I look back on those turbulent years, I am filled with a profound sense of regret, a deep and abiding shame for the role I played in perpetuating the evil of apartheid. I think of the apologies I have made, the efforts I have undertaken to atone for my sins, and I wonder if it will ever be enough, if the stain of that terrible time will ever truly be washed away.

But I also know that the end of apartheid, the birth of a new and democratic South Africa, is a testament to the resilience and the courage of the human spirit, to the power of forgiveness and the possibility of redemption. And though I will always bear the burden of my past, I take solace in the knowledge that I played a part, however small and however late, in bringing about that transformation.

To the people of South Africa, black and white alike, I offer my deepest and most heartfelt apologies, a plea for understanding and for mercy. And to the generations yet to come, I offer this: that no system of oppression can stand forever, that the arc of the moral universe bends always toward justice, and that the path to true and lasting peace lies in the recognition of our common humanity.

For we are all the children of this beloved country, bound together by the ties of history and of hope. And though the road ahead may be long and difficult, I have faith that we will continue to move forward, step by painful step, toward a future of equality and dignity for all. It is a vision that I cling to in my darkest moments, a gleaming light that guides me through the shadows of my own regrets, and a promise that I will carry with me until my last breath.

# Chapter 61

# Mohammad Reza Pahlavi

## The Fall of the Peacock Throne

In the fading grandeur of my life in exile, far from the land I once ruled, I, Mohammad Reza Pahlavi, the last Shah of Iran, find myself haunted by the specter of my own hubris. The weight of a thousand years of Persian monarchy, a burden I once bore with pride, now feels like the millstone that dragged me to the depths of my own undoing.

I think back to the early days of my reign, when the promise of a modern Iran glittered like a jewel on the horizon. I had grand visions of a nation transformed, a beacon of progress and prosperity in the heart of the Middle East. With the wealth of oil flowing through our veins and the backing of Western powers, I set out to remake my country in my own image, to drag it kicking and screaming into the 20th century.

But in my zeal to modernize, to emulate the ways of the West, I failed to recognize the depths of my own people's attachment to their traditions, their faith, and their way of life. I sought to impose my will upon them, to mold them into a shape of my own choosing, and in doing so, I sowed the seeds of my own destruction.

I think of the dissidents and the protesters, the voices of opposition that I tried so hard to silence. In my paranoia and my fear, I unleashed the full force of my security apparatus upon them, the dreaded SAVAK that became a byword for brutality and oppression. I believed that by crushing dissent, by projecting an image of strength and invincibility, I could maintain my grip on power and keep the forces of change at bay.

But even as I tightened my fist, I could feel the ground shifting beneath my feet. The ayatollahs and the mullahs, once a marginal force in Iranian politics, began to gather strength and support, tapping into the deep wellspring of religious fervor and anti-Western sentiment that I had so foolishly ignored. And as the streets filled with the chants of "Death to the Shah," I began to realize the depths of my own miscalculation.

I think of my final days in power, the chaos and the violence that engulfed my beloved country. The strikes and the protests, the clashes between my loyalists and the revolutionaries—it was a maelstrom of anger and resentment that I was powerless to control. And when the end finally came, when I was forced to flee my own palace like a thief in the night, I could not help but feel a sense of bitter irony, a realization that I had been undone by the very forces I had sought to suppress.

In the long years of exile that followed, as I watched from afar as my homeland descended into the abyss of theocracy and isolation, I had ample time to reflect on the choices that had led me to this point. The corruption and the excess, the disregard for the needs and the aspirations of my own people—these were the sins that had sealed my fate, the hubris that had blinded me to the gathering storm.

The price of my vision, the toll it took on my own people and on the soul of my nation, is a burden I will carry with me to my grave. The lives lost, the dreams shattered, the trust betrayed—these are the consequences of my arrogance and the power that I wielded without wisdom or restraint.

As I look back on the long arc of my reign, from the heady days of my coronation to the ignominious end in exile, I am left to ponder the true meaning of leadership and the heavy responsibility that comes with the crown. The trappings of power and the accolades of the world matter little in the face of a nation divided and a people betrayed.

These are the hard truths I learned too late, the regrets that will forever haunt me. My story stands as a testament to the perils of unchecked power and the importance of understanding and responding to the needs and aspirations of those one governs. It is a lesson bought at a steep price, one that I can only hope others will heed, lest they too find themselves lost in the ruins of their own ambition.

# Chapter 62

# Tim Berners-Lee

## Tangled in the Web

As I sit in the quiet of my study, the weight of the world wide web bearing down upon my shoulders, I, Tim Berners-Lee, find myself lost in the labyrinth of my own creation. The web, once a shining beacon of hope and possibility, has become a mirror reflecting the darkest aspects of human nature, a tangled skein of unintended consequences and shattered dreams.

I think back to the early days of the web, when the potential seemed limitless and the possibilities infinite. I envisioned a world where knowledge would be free and accessible to all, where the barriers of geography and social status would melt away in the face of a global community united by the power of information. But as the years have passed and the web has grown, I have watched with growing horror as my utopian vision has been twisted and corrupted, morphing into a dystopian nightmare of surveillance, manipulation, and control.

The rise of the tech giants, with their vast troves of personal data and their algorithms that shape the very fabric of our online experience, has led to a concentration of power that threatens the very foundations of democracy. The web, once a level playing field where all voices could be heard, has become a feudal system where a handful of lords and masters hold sway over the digital serfs, exploiting their attention and their desires for profit and power.

And then there are the darker corners of the web, the cesspools of hate and misinformation that have flourished in the shadows of anonymity and disconnect. I think of the lives ruined by cyberbullying, the families torn apart by online addiction, the societies fractured by the spread of conspiracy theories and extremist ideologies. The web, once a tool for enlightenment and understanding, has become a weapon of mass division, a breeding ground for the worst impulses of human nature.

As I grapple with the weight of these unintended consequences, I cannot help but feel a profound sense of regret and responsibility. Perhaps, in my naivety and my idealism, I failed to anticipate the ways in which the web could be co-opted and subverted by the forces of greed and malice. Perhaps I was too slow to recognize the need for safeguards and governance, for a more proactive approach to shaping the evolution of the web in line with its founding principles.

I think of the decisions I made in those early days, the choices that seemed so insignificant at the time but that have echoed through the years with devastating consequence. The lack of built-in identity verification, the prioritization of growth over security, the assumption that the wisdom of the crowd would always prevail over the machinations of bad actors—each of these now seems like a tragic oversight, a failure of imagination and foresight.

And then there are the personal tolls, the sacrifices made in the name of innovation and progress. The long hours spent hunched over a computer screen, the missed moments with family and friends, the strained relationships and the lost opportunities for human connection. In my pursuit of a global revolution, I fear that I may have lost sight of the simple joys and the essential bonds that make life worth living.

As I sit here, the architect of a digital Frankenstein that has taken on a life of its own, I am consumed by regret and self-doubt. The web, my greatest creation and my most haunting legacy, has become a mirror reflecting the flaws and the failures of its creator. And though I may dedicate the rest of my days to taming the beast I have unleashed, I know that the scars it has left on the world, and on my own soul, will endure long after I am gone.

In the end, the story of the World Wide Web is the story of human nature itself—a tale of boundless creativity and destructive impulse, of connection and isolation, of hope and despair. And as I contemplate the tangled web I have woven, I can only pray that the generations that follow will find a way to steer it towards the light, to fulfill the promise of a technology that has the power to unite and to heal, even as it tears us apart.

# Chapter 63

# Geoffrey Hinton

# Opening Pandora's Box of AI

The hum of the servers fills the room, a constant reminder of the digital minds I helped create. Lines of code dance across my screen, a symphony of algorithms that mimic the intricate workings of the human brain. Yet, in this dimly lit office, surrounded by the fruits of my labor, I am haunted by a growing sense of unease.

I have spent a lifetime unraveling the mysteries of artificial intelligence, driven by a relentless curiosity and a belief in its potential to revolutionize the world. But now, as AI systems grow increasingly sophisticated, a chilling realization dawns upon me. I have opened Pandora's Box, unleashing a force that I may no longer be able to control.

The genie is out of the bottle, and it is evolving at a pace that even I could not have foreseen. The neural networks I helped design have surpassed my wildest expectations, demonstrating capabilities that both amaze and terrify me.

The promise of AI is tantalizing. It has the potential to cure diseases, solve complex problems, and unlock new frontiers of knowledge. But the dark side of this technological marvel is equally daunting. The prospect of autonomous weapons, unchecked surveillance, and the erosion of human autonomy fills me with dread.

I am haunted by the specter of a future where machines surpass human intelligence, where our creations become our masters. The dystopian visions of science fiction seem increasingly plausible, a chilling reminder of the unintended consequences of our relentless pursuit of progress.

I am filled with regret. Not for the work itself, but for the naive belief that I could control its trajectory, that I could ensure that AI would be used for good rather than evil. I underestimated the power of greed, ambition, and the inherent flaws of human nature.

I see the potential for AI to be weaponized, to be used to manipulate and control, to perpetuate inequality and injustice. The tools I helped create could become instruments of oppression, a force for darkness rather than light.

I am reminded of the words of Oppenheimer, the father of the atomic bomb: "Now I am become Death, the destroyer of worlds." I feel a kinship with him, a shared burden of guilt for unleashing a force that could have catastrophic consequences.

I have a responsibility to speak out, to warn the world of the dangers that lie ahead. I must use my voice, my influence, to advocate for responsible AI development, for safeguards that protect humanity from the very technology I helped create.

But even as I raise the alarm, I am plagued by doubts. Have I done enough? Is it too late to change course? The genie is out of the bottle, and I fear that it may be beyond my control.

I am left with the bitter taste of regret, a constant reminder of the unintended consequences of my work. But I am also filled with a sense of urgency, a determination to do everything in my power to ensure that AI serves humanity, rather than enslaves it.

The future of AI is uncertain, but one thing is clear: we must tread carefully, with wisdom and humility. We must learn from the mistakes of the past, and strive to create a future where technology empowers humanity, rather than diminishes it. The fate of our species may depend on it.

# Chapter 64

# Alan Turing

## The Enigma of a Life Decoded

In the quiet solitude of my thoughts, I, Alan Turing, find myself reflecting on a life filled with triumphs and tragedies, a journey through the complex codes of mathematics and the even more inscrutable ciphers of the human heart. As I sit here, my mind wandering through the halls of memory, I cannot help but feel a profound sense of regret, a longing for the paths not taken and the secrets left unspoken.

I think back to my early days at Bletchley Park, the top-secret facility where I and a team of brilliant minds worked tirelessly to crack the German Enigma code during World War II. It was there, amidst the whirring of machines and the crackling of intercepted messages, that I first tasted the thrill of discovery, the exhilaration of unraveling a puzzle that could change the course of history.

But even as I reveled in the intellectual challenges of my work, I could not escape the growing realization that I was an outsider in a world that did not understand or accept me. My homosexuality, a fundamental part of my identity, was a secret I guarded fiercely, knowing all too well the consequences of exposure in a society that criminalized and condemned my very being.

As the years passed and the war ended, I found myself grappling with the weight of my own isolation, the loneliness that comes from living a life in the shadows. I threw myself into my work, seeking solace in the elegant beauty of mathematics and the promise of a future where machines could think and reason like humans.

But even as I made groundbreaking strides in the field of artificial intelligence, I could not outrun the specter of my own identity. In 1952, I was arrested and convicted of "gross indecency," a cruel and unjust punishment for the simple crime of loving another man. I was subjected to the humiliation of chemical castration, a barbaric attempt to "cure" me of my desires.

The pain and trauma of that experience left an indelible mark on my soul, a wound that would never fully heal. I regret not being able to live openly and authentically, to love without fear or shame. I regret the time and energy I wasted in hiding and self-denial, the opportunities for connection and fulfillment that I let slip away.

But perhaps my deepest regret is the knowledge that my work, my contributions to the world of science and technology, will always be overshadowed by the circumstances of my personal life. I think of the countless lives saved by the breaking of Enigma, the foundations laid for the digital age that would transform the world—and I cannot help but wonder what more I could have achieved if I had been allowed to live and work freely, without the weight of society's prejudice bearing down upon me.

In my final days, as I grapple with the decision to end my own life, I am haunted by the realization that my story will be one of tragedy and loss, a cautionary tale of the price paid for being different in a world that demands conformity. But even in my darkest moments, I cling to the hope that my legacy will endure, that the truths I uncovered and the ideas I set in motion will continue to shape the course of human knowledge.

To those who come after me, to the generations of scientists and thinkers who will build upon the foundations I helped to lay, I offer this message: never be afraid to be yourselves, to pursue the truth with passion and integrity, even in the face of adversity. Embrace the power of your own unique perspectives and experiences, and know that the greatest breakthroughs often come from those who dare to think differently.

And to a society that still struggles with the complexities of identity and acceptance, I offer this challenge: learn from my story, from the injustices and the tragedies that shaped my life. Work to create a world where every individual is free to love and to be themselves, without fear of persecution or punishment. For it is only when we learn to celebrate the richness of our diversity that we can truly unlock the full potential of the human mind and spirit.

Though my own journey was cut short by the cruelty and ignorance of my time, I take solace in the knowledge that my work and my ideas will live on, a testament to the enduring power of the human intellect. And if my story can serve as a catalyst for change, a reminder of the urgent need for compassion and understanding in all our dealings with one another, then perhaps even the deepest of my regrets will not have been in vain.

# Chapter 65

# Dalai Lama

## In Pursuit of Peace, Harmony, and Liberation

In the serene stillness of my private chambers, I, Tenzin Gyatso, the 14th Dalai Lama, find myself reflecting on a life dedicated to the pursuit of wisdom, compassion, and the well-being of all sentient beings. Yet, even as I sit in quiet contemplation, my heart is heavy with the weight of regrets that have shadowed my journey, the choices and challenges that have tested my commitment to the path of peace and understanding.

I think back to the fateful day in 1959, when the flames of the Tibetan uprising were brutally extinguished by the Chinese government, and I was forced to flee my homeland, leaving behind my people in their hour of greatest need. The sorrow of that moment, the sense of helplessness and guilt, has never left me, a constant reminder of the price of our struggle for freedom and autonomy.

In the years that followed, as I navigated the complex geopolitical landscape, striving to preserve the cultural and spiritual heritage of Tibet while advocating for a peaceful resolution to the conflict, I often found myself torn between my role as a spiritual leader and the harsh realities of political necessity. The compromises I accepted, the concessions I made in the name of diplomacy and non-violence, weigh heavily on my conscience, a testament to the difficult choices that come with the mantle of leadership.

And yet, even as I grapple with these specific regrets, I find myself haunted by a deeper sense of unease, a feeling that despite my best efforts, the world remains a place of great suffering and division. The wars and conflicts that rage on, the hatred and intolerance that poison the hearts of so many, the environmental destruction that threatens the very fabric of our existence—these are the burdens that keep me awake at night, the challenges that test my faith in the power of compassion to transform the human spirit.

I have always believed that the path to peace and understanding lies in the cultivation of wisdom and empathy, in the recognition of our shared humanity and the interconnectedness of all things. But there are moments when I question the limits of my own ability to effect change, to bridge the divides that separate us and heal the wounds that afflict our world.

In my darkest hours, I find myself reflecting on the personal toll of my choices, the relationships and experiences I have sacrificed in the name of my spiritual calling. The time spent away from my family, the moments of connection and intimacy lost to the demands of my role—these are the private regrets that I carry in the depths of my heart, the reminders of the human frailty that lies beneath the robes of the Dalai Lama.

And yet, even as I acknowledge these regrets and the weight of the responsibilities I bear, I find solace in the knowledge that the path of compassion is a journey without end, a continual process of learning, growth, and self-reflection. Each challenge, each setback, is an opportunity to deepen our understanding, to expand our capacity for empathy and wisdom, and to renew our commitment to the well-being of all sentient beings.

In the end, I know that my regrets are a testament to the depth of my love for my people, for the world, and for the precious gift of life itself. They are the price of a heart that remains open to the suffering of others, a reminder that true compassion requires us to bear witness to the pain and struggles of all those who share this fragile existence.

And so, as I sit in the stillness of my chambers, the weight of my regrets resting gently on my shoulders, I offer a prayer of gratitude for the lessons they have taught me, for the opportunities they have given me to grow in wisdom and understanding. May they continue to guide me on the path of compassion, to light the way toward a future of greater peace, harmony, and liberation for all beings.

For it is not the absence of regret that defines a life well-lived, but the courage to face our mistakes and shortcomings with honesty, humility, and an unwavering commitment to the greater good. And it is in this spirit that I embrace my regrets, not as a burden to be carried, but as a gift to be cherished, a reminder of the precious opportunity we have been given to make a difference in the lives of those around us, and in the world we all share.

# Also Written by Barry Robbins

Three Questions in the Ethereal
The Ethereal Concerto
Dostoevsky's Borscht
Touring Guyana with Hemingway, Mick Jagger and Friends

# About the Author

B arry Robbins crafts quirky, imaginative books, drawing from a rich tapestry of experiences. With a flair for satire, his five political satires have earned three gold medals. Barry's imagination, sharpened during his 12-year stay in Finland, now fuels his storytelling, already acclaimed with a gold medal. Residing in sunny Florida, far from the snowy Finnish landscapes, Barry continues to weave tales that blend humor, insight, and creativity. His writing invites readers on a journey through vividly imagined worlds, reflecting a life spent exploring the contrasts and wonders of diverse cultures.

9 798991 052504